Been So Long III

(Whatever It Takes)

Adrienne Thompson

Pink Cashmere Publishing

Arkansas, USA

Edited by Alyndria Mooney

Cover Design by Adrienne Thompson

Cover Art from dreamstime.com

Printed in the United States of America

First Printing 2014

ISBN: 0988871351

ISBN-13: 978-0-9888713-5-9

Also by Adrienne Thompson:

The *Bluesday* Series:

Bluesday

Lovely Blues

Blues In The Key Of B

The *Been So Long* Series:

Rapture

Been So Long

Little Sister

Been So Long 2

Stand-alone books:

When You've Been Blessed (Feels Like Heaven)

See Me

Your Love Is King

Anthology:

Just Between Us (Inspiring Stories by Women)

Contributed work: "*Epiphany*"

Acknowledgements

Dear Lord,

Thank You so very much for blessing me with this gift. Thank You for allowing me to share it with others. Thank You just for being You. I can never thank You enough.

To my readers:

I wrote *Been So Long* during the winter months of 2011. I had just moved to a new town and was trying to adjust to the changes in my life. Writing about Mona and Corey and Wasif was not only fun for me, it was actually therapeutic, and it helped to relieve some of the loneliness and anxiety I was experiencing at the time.

I never meant for this to be a series. I never expected the books to be so well-received. I surely never expected to sell tens of thousands of books. All I can say is, "but God."

Thank you for embracing Mona-Lisa, flaws and all, and thank you to each and every one of you who have enjoyed reading this series. I truly appreciate you and I mean that from the bottom of my heart. God bless you all.

RIP Nelson Mandela

"Blessed is the man who perseveres under trial…"

James 1:12 NIV

Soundtrack provided by Anita Baker:

"Mystery"

"Watch Your Step"

"Serious"

"Sometimes I Wonder Why"

"Feel The Need"

"No One In The World"

"Been So Long"

"Wrong Man"

"Body And Soul"

"I Can't Sleep"

"Men In My Life"

"Just Because"

"Plenty Of Room"

"In My Heart"

"Lately"

"Caught Up In The Rapture"

"Talk To Me"

"Whatever It Takes"

Soundtrack continued:

"More Than You Know"

"Only For A While"

"Angel"

"Soul Inspiration"

"Moondance"

"Rules"

"Sometimes"

"No One To Blame"

"It's Been You"

"Love You To The Letter"

Prologue

I hurried through the parking lot to the ER entrance, my feet trying to match the pace of my thoughts, which were racing at break-neck speeds—thoughts of the possibilities of what I was to face inside of that hospital. All they'd told me was that my husband was hurt and in critical condition.

I tried to steady my breathing as I held the bottom of my swollen belly and waddled to the receptionist's desk to ask about my husband. Sahib stood behind me, tears streaming down his face. I'd apologized for raising my voice at him, but he had been dragging his feet back at the house and we didn't have time to waste. His feelings were still hurt, but I knew he'd get over it. Besides, what was going on with the love of my life was the most important thing in the world at that moment.

"Please have a seat, ma'am. They're working on your husband right now. I'll let you know his status as soon as I hear from the doctor," the receptionist said in a calm, soothing voice.

I wanted to yell at her, to scream that I didn't want to sit down or wait. I needed to see my husband and I needed to see him RIGHT NOW. I couldn't wait. I had to see his face, to know he was okay. But I looked down at Sahib and then felt my unborn child kick and felt the discomfort I'd been feeling at the bottom of my stomach since I got the news and I decided to go ahead and sit down for a moment.

I took at seat. Sahib sat down beside me and continued to wipe his own tears and sniffle and hiccup air. I pulled him close to me and hugged him tightly. "I'm sorry, baby. Everything will be okay. Stop crying, sweetheart." I kissed his forehead and he began to calm a *bit. That made one of us. I was still on edge, but I knew I had to keep my cool for Sahib and my baby and my husband.*

Thirty minutes of worrying and praying passed and the receptionist finally called my name. She agreed to keep Sahib at her desk for me. As I walked through the ER to Trauma Room 3, I felt my heart race. She'd said he was stable but that I would only be allowed to see him for a moment before they transported him to ICU.

I walked into the room and gasped. There he lay, still—machines whirring all around him. His clothes cut to shreds and in a bloody pile on the floor. I slowly walked over to him and rested my hand on his forehead. I leaned over and kissed his cheek and let my tears flow freely.

"Baby, it's me. It's Mona-Lisa. Please be okay, baby," I whispered. "Please be okay. I need you. We all need you. I can't have this baby alone. Please get better. Please be okay. I love you so much…"

"Mrs. Masood?" A nurse said. "We need to take him to his room now. You can visit him there when he gets settled."

I nodded. "Okay, thank you." I leaned over and kissed his cheek. "I love you, Wasif. I'll see you again really soon."

1

"Mystery"

I bolted upright in the bed. I had been having the same dream every night for more than a week and it was really starting to bother me. I sat there and stared into the darkness, wondering what the dream meant.

Corey sat up next to me, half asleep and half awake. He reached for me and groggily said, "You okay? Is it the baby?" Almost automatically, his hand rested on my stomach and the baby kicked in response.

"No, I just... I have to pee."

"Oh, okay." Corey fell back onto his pillow. I climbed out of bed and headed to the bathroom.

I sat on the toilet and stared at the floor, my mind on the dream— the dream I was too afraid to tell Corey about. The dream I didn't understand but kept having night after night. Why was Wasif my husband in this dream? Where was Corey? Why was Wasif always hurt, at death's door, really? What did the dream mean? I flushed the empty toilet, ran some water in the sink, and then returned to bed. I snuggled close to Corey and closed my eyes, hoping that the rest of my night would be a dreamless one.

***

"You had the dream again?" Cleo asked.

I leaned back in my chair. "Yes. That dream is haunting me. You think it's a warning or something? Should I tell Wasif about it?"

"Only if you plan to tell Corey."

"You know I can't tell him. We've worked hard over these past two years to repair our marriage. I can't tell him I keep having dreams about being Wasif's wife. I'm trying to stay married, Cleo."

"Mo, he can't hold a dream against you. You have no control over your dreams."

"I know that."

"Corey knows it, too."

I sighed. "Look, I can't tell him I'm dreaming about the one man he despises. The man I betrayed him with not once, but *twice*. He might think I'm having some kind of subconscious affair with Wasif or something. Unh-uh. Can't do it."

"Mo, you've got to tell him. If you feel like this is a warning, you've also got to tell Wasif. But you know you can't call Wasif without Corey's knowledge. Wasn't that the agreement?"

"Do you have to be right all of the time?"

"No, but I have to tell you the truth all of the time."

I smiled as I saw the manager's door swing open. "Gotta go. The boss is coming."

"Well, tell the boss I said, hi."

"Will do."

I hung up the phone and said, "Good morning, boss man."

Corey smiled down at me before taking a seat on the edge of my desk. "Good morning, yourself. Feeling okay?"

I nodded. "I'm fine. Feeling even better since you decided to come by and visit us," I said as I patted my stomach.

He leaned over and kissed my forehead. "You know how hard it is for me to sit in that office knowing that the most beautiful woman in the world, the woman who is carrying my child, is just a few feet away from me?"

I stood from my desk and hugged him. "About as hard as it is for me to sit here knowing you're in that office."

He kissed me softly. "Man, you working here at the gym with me was the best decision we've ever made."

I looked into his eyes. "Speak for yourself. The best decision I've ever made was marrying you. I love you so much."

He smiled and pulled me closer to him. "I'm glad to know that because I love you, too."

We kissed for a long, lingering moment, both of us oblivious to the patrons that entered or left the club until the sound of an over-exaggerated "harrumph" brought us out of our bliss.

We both looked up to see Frederick, one of Corey's former coworkers and also one of his first clients, standing at the desk, grinning. "Ain't that how y'all got that one?" he asked, pointing at my stomach.

Corey nodded with a huge grin on his face. "As a matter of fact, we got that one right in my office."

Frederick shook his head. "You two are something else. How are you, Mrs. Sanders?"

I reclaimed my seat and watched as Frederick swiped his gym membership card. "I'm great. Only got seven weeks to go."

"And he's still got you working? Man, what a slave driver." He gave me a wink and then headed off to the locker room.

Corey turned back to me. "He's a nut." He kissed my cheek and as he headed back to his office said, "I'll be right in here if you need me."

"Um, Corey," I said, stopping him in his tracks. "I need to talk to you later... when you're not busy."

He frowned. "Is everything okay? Is there something you're not telling me about you or the baby?"

"No... no, we're fine. It's not that important. It can wait, but I do need to tell you."

"Okay, tell me over lunch."

"Okay."

Lunch seemed to come much sooner than it did on other days. I sighed as I checked my watch and then left the bathroom to make my way to Corey's office. I tapped lightly on his door and then opened it to find him on the phone. He looked up at me, smiled, and nodded towards the chair opposite his desk as he held up a finger and continued his conversation.

As I unpacked the lunches I'd prepared for us that morning, I took in my surroundings. His desk was almost completely covered with neat stacks of computer printouts, membership applications, and bank deposit slips. For a little over two years, Corey had worked tirelessly to build up his clientele and his business. And with my help, he went from working alone with a handful of clients to employing a staff of ten trainers and workout instructors.

The Body Temple was a full-service fitness club complete with daily aerobics classes as well as one-on-one personal training. Now, Corey only trained a few VIP clients himself and spent most of his time handling the business end of things. I worked the front desk and handled the books and some of the marketing. We were a good combination and, together, we kept the club afloat.

Corey ended the call and with excitement in his eyes said, "We are getting closer and closer to becoming a franchise, baby. The guy in Little Rock I told you about is just about ready to sign off on the agreement."

"Really, he's going to sell you his gym? Equipment and all?"

He nodded. "I think so."

"That's great, baby!"

"Yeah, I'm excited about it but enough business talk. I want to hear about you. How are you, baby?"

I took a bite of my sandwich. "Baby, I'm fine. You have got to stop worrying about me. When we agreed to have another child we said we'd trust God to take care of things, remember?"

"I know, I just can't help it. If anything happened to you or the baby I just don't know what I'd do."

I cocked my head to the side. "What happened to the man of God I married? The one who taught me about trust and belief? Where is he?"

"Dang, when you put it that way… okay, you're right. I'm sorry. I just don't want anything to go wrong. I would feel like it was my fault."

"Um, the last time I checked, it took two to make a baby. You are only half-responsible for the creation of this little girl."

Corey smiled. "*A girl*. Man, what am I gonna do with another *you*? And how am I gonna handle her dating? If she looks like you, I'll have to beat the guys off with a stick!"

I laughed. "You've got to survive potty training before you start thinking that far ahead."

He chuckled. "Hey, I can handle it. I handled it with Sahib, didn't I? This ain't my first rodeo, either."

I nodded. "I know it's not."

We were both silent as we dug into our lunches, refueling for the rest of the work day. We were finishing up when I placed my hand on my stomach and smiled. Our little girl was kicking up a storm.

"Is she kicking?" Corey asked as he stood and walked around the desk. He squatted beside me and laid his hand on my stomach. "Wow, she must've liked lunch."

"Yeah, I guess so."

He looked up at me and smiled. "Thank you."

I frowned slightly. "For what?"

"For everything. When we first got back together, I really wasn't sure things would work out, but you have been a wonderful wife. You make me feel like a king, baby. *Thank you.*" He reached up and kissed me gently.

I smiled down at him. "If I wasn't as big as two houses right now, I would insist you put on my favorite uniform and I would tear you up right there on that desk," I whispered.

He raised his eyebrows. "I can lock that door right now. I can work around that belly. You *know* I can."

"Don't play with me, Coach Sanders."

He stood to his feet and walked over to the door. After he locked it, he pulled his Body Temple Polo shirt over his head and in no time, he was in my favorite uniform—minus the whistle. After he helped me out of my clothes, he worked around my belly like a pro.

2

"Watch Your Step"

The day and evening had been so busy that I'd actually forgotten about the dream. But as I climbed into bed next to Corey, it came rushing back to me. And so did the realization that I needed to tell Corey about it. As he settled into his side of the bed, I turned and stared at him for a moment. I silently prayed that he wouldn't take what I was about to tell him the wrong way.

After he turned the lamp off and pulled me into his arms, I said, "Remember I said I needed to tell you something?"

"Oh, yeah. You were supposed to tell me over lunch but we got... uh, sidetracked. Wanna tell me now?"

I sighed. "Not really. But I need to."

The lamp popped back on and Corey sat up in the bed, his eyes glued to mine. "What is it?" he asked softly.

I studied him for a moment, sensing tension from him. "It's nothing bad. It's... I've been having this recurring dream and I... I feel like you should know about it."

"Okay?" he said with a furrowed brow.

I took a deep breath and then recounted my dream for him. I ended with, "I don't know what upsets me more about it, the fact that Wasif is so badly hurt or the fact that he is my husband in the dream."

He nodded. "You think this dream is some kind of forewarning or something?"

I shrugged. "I don't know, but I feel like I need to tell him about it. I just didn't want to talk to him until I talked to you."

Corey sighed. "I'm glad you told me about it. The thing is, I've been having the same dream."

I sat up next to him, my eyes wide. "You have?!"

"Yeah. I didn't know what to do about it. I mean, you know how I feel about him, but the boys love him and for that reason, I wouldn't want something like that to happen to him. You should tell him."

"You really think so?"

"Yeah. If we didn't hate each other, I'd tell him. But as it stands, I don't think he'd listen to me."

I was so relieved. "Is it okay if I call him now? I need to get it off my chest."

Corey handed me his cell phone. "Go ahead."

I kissed his cheek and began to dial the number. A few seconds later, Wasif answered with an uncertain, "Hello?"

"Hey, Wasif? It's Mo. Did I disturb you?"

"Uh... no. Is Sahib okay? What's going on?" Considering the fact that we rarely spoke anymore, his reaction wasn't surprising to me.

"He's fine. He's looking forward to spending next weekend with you."

"Oh... are *you* okay?"

"I'm fine. I actually... I need to talk to you about something."

"Okay, go ahead."

"It can wait if you're busy."

"No, I'm at the hospital but I have a minute. What's on your mind?"

"Okay, well, I've been having this dream…" I described the dream to him and his end of the phone fell silent.

Finally he said, "You think this dream is going to come true or something? "

"I'm not saying that. I just think you should be careful. I felt like I needed to tell you, that's all."

"I see. And I was your husband in the dream?"

Oh, boy, here we go. "Yes."

"Well, I guess the fact that you had a dream about me means we still have a connection, huh?"

I looked over at Corey whose eyes were trained on me. "Of course we do. Morgan and Blair and Sahib are that connection. Look, I'll let you go now. I just wanted you to know."

"Did you know that I'm engaged?" he asked out of the blue.

I frowned a little and kept my eyes in front of me. "W… what?"

"I'm engaged to be married. I thought you should know."

"Oh, well, congratulations."

"Thank you."

"Well, I gotta go. Goodnight, Wasif."

"Goodnight and thank you for your concern."

I ended the call and handed Corey the phone. "What were the congratulations for?" he asked.

"He's engaged," I said. "I didn't see that coming."

Corey turned the lamp off and slid back down in the bed. "Good. Glad to hear he's moving on with his life. Maybe he'll stay out of ours."

I nodded as I rested in his arms. But I honestly didn't know how I felt about it.

***

I had the dream again. The *same* dream—me rushing into the ER, Sahib in tears, the two of us waiting in the lobby, Wasif critically injured. It was so upsetting to me that the dream had not gone away that I ended up staying home from work the next day. Of course this worried Corey and it took so long for me to assure him nothing was wrong with me other than tiredness that he was late getting to the gym.

Around noon, he came home to check on me and announced that he wanted me to stop working altogether until after the baby was born. He said he'd already talked to Tina, our part-time office worker, about working full-time. I didn't argue with him because, honestly, I was tired. I'd miss seeing him throughout the day, but staying home sounded great to me.

That afternoon, Corey called to let me know he was going to watch Frederick's basketball game and would be home a little after 9:00 P.M. that evening. Frederick coached basketball at one of the local high schools.

"Oh, well, it'll be lonely here with just me and Sahib," I whined.

"Aw, baby. Frederick just wants me to sit on the bench with him and give him some pointers. I promised him I'd make a game this season."

"I know but I'll still miss you."

"You don't want me to go? Say the word and I'll come home."

I sighed. "No, I wouldn't want you to disappoint Frederick."

"You sure?"

"Yeah. It's a pity, though. I was hoping you'd work around my stomach again."

"What time did I say I'd be home?"

"After 9:00 P.M."

"Make that 8:30 P.M."

"Will the game be over by then?"

"It will for me. I ain't missing out on a chance to work around your stomach. Love you, baby. See you tonight."

I smiled. "Okay. Love you, too."

I picked Sahib up from school, cooked dinner, talked to my sister on the phone, watched a little television, and around 8:30 P.M., settled into bed for the night. I was too tired to wait another minute for Corey to make it home. He'd just have to wake me up. I prayed that the dream would not disturb my rest that night, and after settling underneath the covers, I fell into a glorious, dreamless sleep.

I woke up around midnight to find myself alone in bed. After rushing to the bathroom to empty my bladder, I walked through the house and checked for any sign of Corey. He wasn't there. His car wasn't in the driveway and calls to his cell phone went unanswered. I sat on the side of my bed and tried to figure out what to do next or who to call. Frederick?

As my mind raced with thoughts—some strategic, others troubling—my cell phone rang and Corey's number flashed across the screen. I answered it with an eager "Corey, where are you? Are you okay?"

"Mrs. Sanders?" The voice on the other end was not my husband's.

"Who is this?" I asked, panic heightening and quickly replacing any semblance of rationality left in my mind.

"I'm trying to reach a Mrs. Corey Sanders?" He sounded official, too official—like a police officer or something. Something was wrong. Something had happened. *No… no… no…*

"This is she. Who-is-this?"

"Mrs. Sanders, we found this phone on your husband's person and—"

"Found? What the hell is going on? Where is my husband?!"

"Ma'am, please try to stay calm."

I closed my eyes, sucked in a breath, and as I released it, tried to calm my throbbing heart. "Please tell me what's going on."

"Ma'am, there was an incident at the Conway High School gym tonight."

"An incident? What do you mean?"

"Mrs. Sanders, there was a shooting and several people were

injured... including your husband."

3

"Serious"

I felt like I was watching myself as I snatched my youngest son out of bed and shoved his shoes onto his feet. I nearly lost it when he crawled back into bed. I felt bad as tears flooded his little cheeks while I put his jacket on him and zipped it over his pajama top. I threw a coat on over my rumpled ensemble of one of Corey's t-shirts and a pair of maternity jeans, let my dog out into the back yard, and then dragged Sahib out of the house to my car. I don't recall the drive from my home to the hospital. Time seemed to lapse between me sticking the key in the ignition and screeching to a halt in front of the ER entrance.

Deja vu invaded every inch of me as I rushed to the receptionist and stammered out my husband's name.

"C... Corey Sanders? He's hurt. He's here. He's my husband," I said, my thoughts spewing out of my mouth in no particular order.

She checked the computer with no sense of urgency—like she was checking to see if there were any rooms available in a hotel.

I leaned against the desk and tightened my grip on Sahib's hand and bit my tongue. I closed my eyes and moved my free hand to my stomach, trying to relieve the pressure that had come and gone from the moment I received that phone call.

"Okay, they're still working on him," she finally said. "Please have a seat and I'll call you as soon as he can have visitors."

I opened my mouth to say something ugly then decided against it. If they were back there helping Corey, I didn't want to interfere with that. So I nodded and whispered a weak "thank you" before leading Sahib to a seat. I sat down and tried to comfort him as my heart thundered in my chest and my unborn child rolled and tumbled inside of me. I needed to call the twins and Corey's parents and my sister but first, I needed to see him, to know that he was okay. I needed to walk into the trauma room and see the familiar scene that had haunted my dreams—the machines, the bloody clothes, my husband lying there helpless and still, but alive. The dream had been a warning all right, but the casting was off. Instead of Wasif, it was Corey who was fighting for his life.

I closed my eyes and thought of the last words I'd heard him say. *"Love you, baby. See you tonight."*

I felt a tear escape my eye and slide down my cheek. If I'd known the dream was really about him, I would've insisted he come home... or would I? The dream didn't give any details about the cause of the injuries. No, there probably wasn't anything I could've done to stop it. Nothing at all.

I told myself that at least the dream had given me a sort of advantage. At least I already knew he'd be okay. I knew I'd be able to see him and to touch him soon. Those realizations seemed to calm me a bit, and I began to relax in my seat. The pressure I'd been feeling in my stomach ceased.

I had closed my eyes and was still holding Sahib in my arms when I heard a voice call my name. But something was not right. It wasn't the receptionist's voice I heard, but a male voice. I opened my eyes to see a police officer standing over me, a solemn look on his face. I stood from my seat. Sahib stood next to me.

"Mrs. Sanders?" he repeated.

I nodded slightly. "Yes," I said weakly.

"I'm Officer Ryan. I'm the one who called you to let you know about your husband. I hear they're still working on him?"

I nodded again.

"I need to give these to you." I looked down at his hand and saw that he was holding Corey's cell phone and wallet. I took them from him.

"Thank you," I said softly. I hated the sound of my own voice. I sounded so small, so defeated.

The officer nodded. "No problem, ma'am. I really hope your husband pulls through. By all accounts, he was a hero tonight."

I looked up at the officer through dry eyes. "He was?"

"Oh, yes, ma'am. When the shooting started, he was sitting on the coach's bench. I hear that he helped save some of the kids' lives."

That sounded like Corey. He loved children, and he'd never hesitate to protect them. "Was anyone else shot?" I asked.

"Yes, ma'am. Eight people in all. Three adults, five children."

"Was… was anyone killed?"

The officer closed his eyes and hesitated before saying, "Yes, ma'am. Three people. The coach for the home team, a Mr. Frederick Morton, and two students."

I gasped. "Frederick? Frederick is… dead? *Why?* Why did this happen?"

The officer shook his head. "We're not sure yet, ma'am, but we know who did this. There were several witnesses and I'm confident that we will be making an arrest soon. I am very sorry, ma'am."

I nodded and took my seat as the officer walked away. Several minutes passed and just as I was about to approach the receptionist's desk again, she finally called my name.

I walked over to the desk and anxiously said, "Yes? Can I go back and see him now?"

She gave me a sympathetic look. "Actually, Mrs. Sanders, one of the physicians who've been working on your husband would like to speak to you." Did that damn dream get anything right?

I sighed, felt pressure build up in my head instead of my stomach, and said, "Okay."

"Come with me," she said as she stood from her seat and began to lead me to the doors that led into the ER unit.

"Can my son come back, too? I don't have anyone here with me to watch him."

She smiled warmly. "He can stay with me."

She escorted me to an empty room and I bent over and kissed Sahib's forehead. "You go with the nice lady, okay? I'll see you in a little bit. Be a good boy."

I could see big crocodile tears forming in his eyes as he nodded and took the receptionist's hand. I made a mental note to call Wasif after I spoke with the doctor to see if he could pick Sahib up. I sat there in that little room for what felt like days before the door swung open to reveal none other than Wasif, dressed in scrubs, a haggard look on his face.

I hopped up and rushed to meet him in the small space. "W… what are you doing here? What's going on?"

Wasif's eyes took me in, lingering at my stomach as he began to speak. "I'm the on-call cardiothoracic surgeon for tonight. They called me in because Sanders was shot in the chest—twice. The bullets have torn through his thoracic cavity. There's been extensive damage to a lot of blood vessels, there's a bullet in one of his lungs, and his aorta was nicked. He's lost a lot of blood. "

"Wasif, what the hell does all of that mean?!" I asked, my composure eroding at a maddening pace.

"It means he needs surgery, Mo, and he needs it *now*. Look, they called me in to do it, but I can't. I've called another surgeon and he'll be here within the hour. He's driving in from Little Rock."

I gripped my now pounding head. "What? I don't understand. If he needs it now, can he wait for the other surgeon to get here?"

"Well, right now he's holding on. They're keeping him as stable as they can."

"But there's a chance he won't make it?"

"Well, of course with cases like this, the sooner he gets into surgery the better. His chances of surviving diminish with every minute that passes."

"Then why don't you just go ahead and do the surgery?"

"You *know* why. We have history. There's a huge conflict of interest here."

My eyes searched his. "Please, don't do this to me, to Corey. I know you hate him, but he is Morgan's father and Sahib and Blair love him and I am carrying his child right now. I *need* him, Wasif. Please help him. *I am begging you.*"

Wasif gripped the back of his own neck and began to pace the room. "Mo… this isn't about my personal feelings. It's just not a good idea for me to do this. What if something goes wrong? You'll swear I *tried* to hurt him. I could be brought up on malpractice charges. I'm sorry. I just can't do it."

That's when my desperation transformed into anger. "Wasif, my husband is in there about to die and every reason you've given me for not helping him has been a selfish one. I am asking you right now as a woman you once loved to do this for *me*. If you ever really loved me at all, if you ever cared about me, you will help him. *Please*."

Wasif stared at me. I could see the wheels turning in his head and I knew what he was going to say before he said it.

"I still love you."

I closed my eyes and sighed. "Wasif, not now."

"No, listen. You said if I ever loved you. I still love you, Mo."

I opened my eyes and looked up at him. "If you really mean that, you will do the surgery."

"I can't."

"What do you want me to do? Fall on my knees and plead? Just tell me, and I'll do it. Please, Wasif. I am begging you. *Please*."

He stared at me for a long, excruciating moment. Tears I'd been holding back flooded my face. I leaned against the wall, hung my head, and whispered, "Oh, God, please help me."

"Mo..."

I turned my face to the wall and sobbed loudly. *He's going to let him die. He's not going to help him,* I thought.

"Mo, the other surgeon is on the way and he—"

I turned to face him. I glared at him as I wiped my tear-drenched face. "I don't give a damn about the other doctor! *You're* here. You could help him but you won't. If he doesn't make it, I will never forgive you. Do you understand me? *Never!*" I moved towards the door and he blocked me. "Get out of my way!" I hissed.

"I'll do it," he said softly.

"What?"

"I... I said I'll do it."

"You will?"

"Yes."

I fell against him and hugged him tightly. "Thank you, Wasif. Thank you so much."

"Mo, if something goes wrong..."

"Nothing will go wrong. I trust you. Thank you so much."

"Yeah, well, you can see him for a few seconds then we'll need to get him prepped for surgery."

"Okay. Thank you, again."

Wasif led me to Corey, to Trauma Room 3, and there I saw the same scene from my dream with Corey's powerful body replacing Wasif's. I walked over to him and gently rubbed my hand across his cheek. I kissed his eyelids and then his lips. "I love you, baby. Hold on okay? You're gonna be okay but you've got to hold on. I love you so much." I closed my eyes and silently prayed for him as I held his hand in mine.

A minute or so later, a nurse came in and asked me to leave. It was time to prep Corey for surgery. I kissed him one last time, told him I loved him again, and then left. Out in the lobby, I retrieved my son and called my sister. I told her about Corey and asked her to call the twins and gave her Corey's parents' number so that she could call them, too. Then I went to the chapel to pray.

It was in the chapel that the pressure in my stomach turned into pain. The pain was so sudden and intense that all I could do was close my eyes and try to remember to breathe. Once it was over, I told myself that this couldn't be happening. It was too early and just out-and-out inconvenient. I could *not* go into labor. I needed to be by Corey's side after the surgery. I needed to know what was happening as it happened.

I sat still and waited for another pain. Sahib tugged on my coat sleeve. "Are you okay, Mommy?" he asked.

I reached over and dug my fingers into his thick hair. I gave him a reassuring smile and said, "I'm fine. Are you okay?"

He closed his eyes and shook his head. "No. I'm sleepy."

I gathered him in my arms and he rested his head against my stomach. "I know. I'm sorry. I'm going to take you back home as soon as I know Coach is okay. I promise."

"Okay."

We left the chapel and headed through the hospital to the empty surgery waiting room.

4

"Sometimes I Wonder Why"

The wait was agonizingly long and the time that passed was hard to keep track of despite the fact there was a bright, oversized digital clock mounted on the wall of the waiting room. I couldn't concentrate on the changing numbers because my mind was full of thoughts and worries. What if he didn't make it? What would I do without him? Would the little girl in my womb ever know him? Was I really in labor?

The pains came and went—five of them in all. How long had it been? One hour? Two? I looked over at Sahib who was lying across two chairs, fast asleep. I shook my head and whispered, "I'm not in labor."

I whispered the words over and over again as if by merely saying them, I could make them be the truth. In the middle of me reciting my mantra, another pain hit. I bent over a little and braced myself and told myself to breathe. I shut my eyes tightly as I waited for the pain to subside. Then, in my mind, I began to recite my mantra again. *I'm not in labor... I'm not in labor... I'm not in labor...*

"Are you okay?" A voice said. A female's voice. *My sister's voice.*

I opened my eyes and looked at her to be sure my mind wasn't playing tricks on me. "Cleo? You're here?" I looked past her and saw her husband standing right behind her. "Scott?" I whispered. "How'd y'all get here so fast?"

Cleo squatted in front of me and reached for my hand. "Didn't I ever tell you about Scott's lead foot? Girl, he nearly scared me to death, but at least he got us here in record time. I had to be here for you."

I closed my eyes, relief filling my heart. "Thank you so much. I felt so alone here—wait, where are the kids?"

"With Scott's parents. Now I need for you to answer *my* question. Are you okay? You looked like something was wrong a second ago."

"I'm fine now," I said as she reached up and hugged me. "Did you call everyone?"

She nodded as she took a seat across from me. "Yeah, Morgan was pretty upset. He and Blair are on their way."

I rested a hand on Sahib's leg. "Lord, I hope they're careful. If something happens to them I'm gonna lose my entire mind. I don't know how I'm holding it together as it is."

"Because God is helping you," Cleo said.

"Yeah. What about Corey's parents? Were you able to reach them?"

"Yeah. I spoke with his father. They're on their way, too. His father is so nice."

I nodded. "Yeah, Corey's a lot like him. Thank God you didn't talk to his mother. She is a challenge, to say the least."

"She can't be that bad."

"You'll see." I turned to my brother-in-law. "Thank you for bringing her, Scott."

He smiled. "Of course. You're family. Is there anything you need me to do?"

"You did it when you brought my sister here."

"Anything else, you just let me know."

We all sat there and waited together, and I silently thanked God for bringing my little sister back into my life. She was the best part of me, the only good that ever came from my mother.

When I saw Wasif approaching us with a grave look on his face, my heart began to beat in triple time. In my mind, I began to repeat a new set of words: *please, God... please, God... please, God...*

I stood from my seat as if changing my position would make the words I wanted to hear flow from his mouth. He nodded at Cleo and Scott who now flanked me. "Mo," he began. "I tried my best—"

My knees buckled and I would've fallen had Scott not caught me. "Noooo, no, no, no!!!!" I wailed loudly.

Cleo grabbed me and held me and said something to me that I couldn't understand. I could hear Wasif saying something, too, but the raw grief that I felt served to deafen me. I closed my eyes and continued to wail loudly.

Wasif's voice sounded hollow in my ears. "Mo, listen to me!"

Sahib woke up and began to cry.

"Why?!!! Why, Lord?! Why???!!" I continued, tears mingling with snot as I fought to break free from Scott and Cleo. I just wanted to run. There was no destination. I just wanted to run until I ran out of breath, until I collapsed. Another pain hit me and I grabbed my stomach and yelled, "Ohhhhh!!"

"What is it? It's the baby isn't it?" Cleo asked.

I nodded.

"Scott, go get help!" she said.

5

"Feel The Need"

I lay in the hospital bed, unrelenting tears flowing as the nurse wrapped the blood pressure cuff around my arm. I wailed softly, my heart splintering with each beat.

"My goodness, your blood pressure is through the roof! Can you try to calm down, ma'am? You've *got* to calm down."

I nodded and snuffled and said, "I... I'll try. My... my... my hus-husband—h... he d-d-d-died t-tonight—"

"No, sweetie, he *didn't*. Your sister just called back here and asked me to tell you that he's alive."

I shook my head. "N-no, she's just saying that b-because of the b-baby." I snuffled and tried to breathe but then I began to hiccup.

"Mrs. Sanders, please try to calm down. If you don't, the doctor is going to *have* to deliver this baby. Now, the medicine in this IV will stop your labor and it can also lower your blood pressure, but you have to calm down."

I turned my head and closed my eyes and continued to cry. The only thought running through my head was, *What am I going to do now? What am I going to do?* "But, my husband," I said weakly.

"Honey, he's alive."

"I-I don't believe it. If he's alive, I want to see him. I won't believe it until I see for myself."

"Mrs. Sanders, you can't leave this unit in your condition. You are in active labor right now."

My patience was running as thin as my sanity at that point. "Women have babies at home all the time! And you mean to tell me I can't sit in a wheelchair and wheel over to ICU to see my husband? The only way I will be able to calm down is if I see for myself that he is alive."

She sighed. "You can have visitors now. Do you want me to send your family back?"

"I don't care. It doesn't matter."

The nurse left and I tried to heed her warning. The last thing I needed or wanted to happen was for the baby to come early. I tried to calm myself but how could I when the only visions in my mind were of an orderly wheeling my husband's lifeless body to the morgue? I closed my eyes and prayed for God to help me. I prayed that he would take the unbearable ache that seemed to fill every crevice of my heart away. I prayed for my sons, knowing that their hearts would be broken when I told them that Corey was gone. And I prayed for the strength to raise Sahib and my daughter without Corey. How would I ever show my little girl how truly wonderful her father was?

Was.

The thought of referring to my husband in the past tense brought on fresh tears and refueled my agony. Cleo came into the room and rushed to the side of the bed. Any other day, the sight of her beautiful face and her unruly hair would've been enough to lift my spirits. But not today.

"Did the nurse tell you about Corey?" she asked.

I nodded as she gripped my trembling hand. "Yeah, but I don't believe it."

"Mo, I am telling you the truth. You didn't let Wasif finish. Corey is alive—critical, but alive."

"Like I told that nurse, I won't believe it until I see it."

"Mo, you are in a hospital gown, in a hospital bed, in labor weeks before your due date. They are not gonna just let you just walk out of here."

"Hell, I'll go in a wheelchair."

"Mo, the nurse told me about your blood pressure. What you need to do is relax and calm down. You need to stay in that bed."

"The only way I can relax or calm down is to know that my husband is alive."

"He *is*. I'm telling you the truth. Why don't you believe me?"

"Because you are my sister and you love me and I know you would do anything to ease my mind."

"That's all true, but I'm not lying, Mo."

The blood pressure cuff began to inflate on its own. Evidently, the nurse had set it to monitor automatically. When it was done, my blood pressure appeared on the screen. It didn't take a doctor or a nurse to tell that it was sky high.

"Mo! Your blood pressure! You've got to calm down!"

I sat up in the bed. "I can't! My husband is dead, Cleo! *Dead!* How in the hell am I supposed to calm down? Would you be calm if it was Scott? Would you just lie here and take my word for it that he was alive?!"

Cleo sighed. "I'll be right back."

I lay there through another bad blood pressure check before she returned with my nurse and a wheelchair. The nurse handed me a clipboard and a pen. "You can go see your husband, but you have to sign for a discharge against medical advice. We'll have to readmit you when you come back. I'll have to discontinue the IV. Know that this hospital is not responsible for you or your baby after you leave this unit."

"I understand," I said as I signed the paper.

"Please make it as quick as possible, Mrs. Sanders. With your blood pressure like this, you and the baby are truly in danger."

"I understand. I'll be right back."

A couple of minutes later, Cleo wheeled me out of Labor and Delivery. We stopped by the waiting area where Sahib was fast asleep in Scott's lap, and then we made our way through the hallways of the second floor to ICU.

"If anything happens to you or this baby, Corey will never forgive you and neither will I," Cleo whispered.

"I know."

We finally made it to the ICU and after Cleo explained the situation to a nurse, she led us to his room and there, with my own eyes, I saw him—unconscious, but alive. I sat there and rubbed the top of his hand and stared at the rising and falling of his chest for fifteen whole minutes before we had to leave. I felt so relieved. It didn't matter that he was in critical condition. It didn't matter that he wasn't out of the woods. What mattered—*the only thing that mattered*—was that the love of my life, my provider, my protector, was still alive.

I stood from the wheelchair, whispered "I love you," and kissed his cheek. I almost felt normal again and I let a small smile creep upon my lips as I sat back down in the wheelchair. Then, as Cleo wheeled me out of the room, one of the machines began to alarm. A nurse breezed past us and rushed to Corey's bedside screaming, "Code Blue!"

I frowned and felt my chest begin to tighten. "What is it?!" I screamed.

As more nurses entered the room, Corey's nurse screamed, "You need to leave, *now*!!"

Cleo began hurriedly pushing me out of the room even as I yelled at her to stop. Then I felt the worst pain yet—a full-force labor pain. And when the warm fluid gushed from between my legs, I knew I was in trouble.

6

"No One In The World"

Corey didn't get to hold my hand and coach me through my labor. He wasn't there to remind me to breathe. He didn't get to see the baby crown. He didn't get to cut the umbilical cord. Corey didn't get to hold his daughter in the delivery room and it was not Corey who handed her to me.

Only thirty minutes after Cleo rushed me back to labor and delivery, I gave birth to a five pound, six ounce little girl with smooth, brown skin and a head full of fine, black hair. Cleo was by my side the whole time. It was a blessing to be able to share that moment, that event, with my sister and I was thankful for her being there. But I would have given absolutely *anything* to have replaced her with Corey.

I was only able to hold my little girl for a few seconds before they took her from me and rushed her to the neonatal ICU. The doctor said her breathing was off, that her lungs probably hadn't had time to fully develop but that she would, most likely, be fine. By then, I was certain that Corey had died in ICU. All I could do now was pray that God would spare the last piece of Corey I had left besides Morgan— our daughter.

Cleo left to take Sahib home, at my request, but she promised to come right back to check on me and Corey. I was alone when a nurse came in to give me the good news that my blood pressure was beginning to drop. I guess that was because I had moved from hysterics to numbness. I was just too hurt to feel anymore.

I was lying in bed staring at the ceiling when I heard a soft rapping at the door. I shifted my eyes to the door and stared at it but didn't say a word. More rapping, louder and more persistent this time, and just when I decided to say "come in," the door flew open and in came my twins—first Morgan, then Blair and, bringing up the rear, my father or the man I un-affectionately referred to as my mother's sperm donor. The boys rushed to either side of my bed and their questions came in such a rapid-fire manner, I barely had a chance to answer either of them.

"Are you okay? Where is the baby? Where's Sahib? Are they all right?" Blair asked.

Morgan had something else on his mind. "We stopped by and saw Coach in the ICU. Do they know who shot him? Have they caught them? Are they looking for them?"

I answered both of them with, "What the hell is *he* doing here?"

The twins fell silent, their eyes focused on the floor. So I directed my question to my father. "As you can see, I'm in no condition to donate any of my vital organs to you and I wouldn't if I *could*. Hell, I wouldn't give you a kidney even I had *three* of them. So what the hell are you doing here?"

He cleared his throat and swiped at his brow. "Um-well-uh, I... the boys said they needed to come home and they were real upset and I didn't want either of them to drive like that. I didn't want them to have a wreck. Plus, I wanted to be sure you were okay. I was worried."

I stared at him as I stifled a laugh. "Yeah, right. Well, you can go *worry* out in the waiting room while I talk to my sons."

He nodded and ducked out the door without another word.

"He really was worried, Mama," Blair offered.

"Mm-hmm, enough about him. Now to answer your questions, I'm fine. Sahib is at home with your Aunt Cleo and Uncle Scott. The baby's having a little trouble breathing but the doctor thinks she'll be okay. The police are looking for the guy who's responsible for the shooting and Morgan, I see the look in your eyes. You let the police handle this."

Morgan cocked his head to the side. "Yeah, well, they better get to handling it or else I will."

"Morgan, *please*. There is enough bad stuff going on. Do not do this!"

"Okay, okay, I'm sorry. I don't wanna upset you."

"You saw your father? H... how was he?"

Morgan's expression transformed in an instant. Sadness clouded his eyes. "I don't like seeing him like that. All those machines and stuff. I don't like it at all."

"I know. Me either. But at least he's still alive."

Morgan leaned over and rested his head on my chest. Blair walked around the bed and laid his hand on Morgan's back. It made me feel a little better to have my boys there with me, sharing in my pain and giving me their love. I hadn't cried since I saw Corey in ICU, but there with my boys, the floodgates opened once more. And as they comforted me, I wondered if my life would ever be normal again.

***

After three days in the NICU and on oxygen, my little girl was doing better. I finally got to hold her again and kiss her little cheeks and smell her scent, and though I was being discharged that day, I vowed not to spend a night at home until I could take her with me. Corey's parents arrived the day after he was shot and didn't bother to stop by my room to visit me or even check on the baby. They headed straight to ICU where they had been camped out in the waiting area ever since, visiting Corey as often as they were allowed to.

They didn't like me and I knew it, so I was glad to have Cleo and the boys with me when I arrived in the ICU waiting area. We sat across from them and I held my breath as I pulled Sahib onto my lap. I knew Mr. Virgil Sanders didn't care for me but at least he had the decency to fake it. He smiled and spoke to us, giving Morgan, his grandson, a genuine smile. Now, Stella Sanders was a different story. She didn't bother to speak to any of us—not even Morgan. She just sat there and gave me that scowl she always gave me. After all these years, the woman still despised me. Though Corey had forgiven me long ago, she still harbored hard feelings for me for breaking Corey's heart in college since, as far as I knew, she wasn't privy to the details of our separation a couple of years earlier. As a matter of fact, neither of his parents had ever stepped foot in our home and we were never invited to theirs for holidays or birthdays or *any* days.

After far too many uncomfortable minutes passed, she finally said, "How's the baby?" She didn't address me specifically. It was more like she threw the question into the air for anyone to catch.

"Better," I said. "They might release her in a few days."

Another genuine smile from Mr. Sanders. "Well, that's good news. You thought of a name yet?"

I returned his smile. "Well, Corey and I still hadn't decided before... before he was hurt. We thought we had more time to decide. I don't want to name her until he wakes up."

"You're gonna take her home without a name?" Corey's mother asked as if it was the most ridiculous thing she'd ever heard. And maybe it *was* ridiculous, but that's the way things were going to be. Our daughter wasn't going to have a name until her father could name her.

"If I have to. But hopefully it won't come to that. Hopefully, Corey will regain consciousness and be able to name her."

"I think he'll appreciate that," Corey's father said. Stella shot him a displeased look and he dropped his eyes to the floor and slumped back in his seat.

A few seconds later, Wasif walked out of the doors that led into the ICU and approached us. Corey's father stood from his seat and reached for Wasif's hand. "Doc, what's the report for today?" he asked in a friendly tone. As Wasif began to run down Corey's condition—no change, still critical, etcetera, etcetera—I noticed how attentive and receptive Corey's parents were to him, and it occurred to me that they had no idea who he was to me.

After he had finished his official report, he turned to me and smiled as Sahib climbed out of my lap and leaped into his arms. Morgan and Blair both stood and hugged him.

"You okay?" Wasif asked me. "How's the baby?"

"We're okay," I said. Then I glanced at Corey's parents who both wore bewildered expressions. "Mr. and Mrs. Sanders, Dr. Masood is Blair and Sahib's—"

Mrs. Sanders held up a hand to interrupt me and with a sour look on her face said, "I know who he is now. Morgan's brothers look just like him."

Morgan's brothers? It took all of the Jesus I had worked so hard to keep inside of me not to hop up out of my seat and punch her for that smart little remark.

I opened my mouth to say something in rebuttal but Cleo grabbed my hand and squeezed it tightly, reminding me that this woman, however snarky she was being with me, was Corey's mother. I settled back in my seat and returned my attention to Wasif. "Thanks for the progress report. I appreciate everything you've done to help Corey."

"No problem. I'll be by to pick up Sahib in the morning."

I nodded. "If we're not home, we'll be here."

"Okay. Morgan, Blair, you're welcome to spend the weekend at my place, too. I'd love for you to meet Ann." *Ann? Must be his fiancée's name.*

I still wasn't sure how I felt about his engagement, but I had too much going on to really even think about it. Morgan and Blair agreed to visit him and a few minutes after Wasif left, the doors to the ICU swung open indicating that visiting hours, or actually, visiting *minutes* had begun. I joined the exodus of families filing through the doors for the first of four 15-minute visiting sessions in the ICU.

We crowded into Corey's room, all of us wearing forlorn expressions, our minds full of questions that only God could answer. I was the first to approach his bed. I grasped his hand and kissed it as I rubbed my other hand across his forehead and smiled down at him. "We're all here, Corey. The whole family is here and we love you. We're praying for you. Be strong and get well, baby, because we miss you. I miss you so much and I need you. Get well, okay?"

I backed away from the bed and watched as the rest of the family, *our* family, approached the bed and held his hands and talked to him.

I was at every visitation that day. I prayed that very soon, Corey would open his eyes and talk back to us.

I was finally able to take Baby Girl Sanders home after she was forced to spend the first two weeks of her life in the hospital. In just that small amount of time, I could see both myself and Corey begin to show in her. She definitely had my feistiness and my features, and Corey's strength. I felt torn about leaving the hospital, though. My only consolation was that Corey's parents were still camped out in the ICU waiting room, so I knew he wouldn't be alone.

Corey.

There'd been little to no change in him in two weeks. He hadn't regained consciousness. Wasif said he'd lost a lot blood and that it might have affected his brain. His lung had been so badly damaged, it might never work at its full capacity again. He said that when Corey woke up, *if* he ever woke up, he might be handicapped for life. That—*all of that*—scared me. But the thought of losing him scared me more. So I took my little nameless baby home and cared for her and was only able to visit Corey twice a day while Cleo watched her for me. Since Thanksgiving break was in a few weeks, I convinced the twins to go back to school with a promise to keep them updated on Corey's condition and told them to just head back home for the break. My mother's sperm donor, who had left town the day after he arrived, drove back to Conway and picked them up. I was glad he had the good sense not to try to communicate with me again.

I tried to convince Cleo to leave, too, but she refused. She sent her husband home but she stayed right there by my side and though I truly needed her there to help me, a part of me wished to be alone in my sorrow. A part of me needed to be in solitude, to mourn my situation. But more than anything, a part of me wanted to give up hope, because being hopeful was taxing. I was tired of hoping against hope and of trying to keep a positive attitude. I was tired of acting brave and pretending to have faith when the truth was that my faith was on its last leg and my heart had taken so many direct hits, I wasn't sure if it could be repaired. My life just seemed to me to be nothing more than a map of connected tragedies and heartaches.

Reconnecting with Corey had been one of the bright spots in my life. Marrying him had been my greatest accomplishment besides the births of my children. Living with him as his wife was blissful at worst, heavenly at best. But now it seemed that someone had destroyed all of the goodness in my life with a gun and some bullets. Someone who had probably never met Corey and wouldn't recognize him on the street had ruined our lives.

And so the days passed in their usual manner—one by one—until another week had passed and they finally upgraded my husband's condition from critical to serious. Still not out of the woods but a little further down the road than before. As the weeks turned into a month, I began to think about names for the baby. I needed to take her for her shots and there were insurance papers to fill out. So I tried to remember the names we'd discussed. What were his favorites? What were mine? By the end of that night, exactly one month after Corey was shot, I'd compiled a list of names. When I slipped into bed that night, I'd settled on a name for our little girl: Corii.

7

"Been So Long"

It was around 3:00 A.M. when I got the call. I was so deeply asleep that it took a moment for me to realize I was not dreaming—my phone was actually ringing. I glanced over at the bassinette sitting next to the bed before I groped for the phone on the night table. Finally finding it, I answered with a groggy, "Hello?"

"Mona? This is Stella. Corey's awake and he's asking for you!" Corey's mother gushed into my ear.

I sprung from my bed to my feet and stumbled across my dark bedroom to the closet. *Please let me be awake, Lord. Don't let this be a dream. Please, please, please...* "He... he's awake and he's talking?"

"Yes! The nurse came and got us but she said the first word out of his mouth was your name. He's worried about you."

Tears sprung to my eyes as I snatched my thin gown over my head and replaced it with a wrinkled t-shirt. "Oh, thank The Lord! I'm on my way!"

I snatched on a pair of jogging pants and tied a scarf on my head then shoved my feet into a pair of flip-flops. It was cool outside, but I didn't care. I didn't have time to worry about finding proper footwear. My husband was alive and awake! If I had to, I'd go to that hospital in nothing but my bra and panties.

I rushed down the hall to Sahib's room where my little sister was fast asleep. I shook her awake and then began to speak in spewing words. "Cleo, get up. I need you to watch the baby. Corey's awake and he's asking for me and I need to get to the hospital *now*!"

Cleo bolted upright in bed. "What?! Praise God! You go on. I got the baby. I'm so happy for you!!"

I quickly hugged her and then left her in my bedroom with the baby as I headed out the door. I made it to the hospital in record time.

A smile spread across my face as I stepped into the Corey's room. There were no tubes or machines. Only the hum of the electronic blood pressure cuff could be heard. Corey was staring at the ID bracelet on his wrist as I moved closer to the bed.

"Hey, handsome," I said softly. I placed my hand over his.

He turned his head and looked at me. His face read relief. "Hey, baby," he said in a raspy voice. He pulled my hand to his dry lips and kissed it.

"How do you feel?" I asked.

"Like I've been shot," he answered wryly.

I smiled. "Good answer." I leaned over and kissed him. "You know, if you were a rapper, this would give you so much street cred'."

He smiled and then grimaced as if the smile had hurt him. "Yeah, not a good look for a fitness trainer, huh?" He shook his head. "How do *you* feel?" he asked, then looked down at my stomach and gave me a panicked look. "The baby?"

Nobody's told him, I thought. I looked him in the eye and said, "The baby's fine. She's perfect, Corey."

"You already had her?!" He placed his hand on his forehead. He turned his face towards me and I could see tears welling up in his eyes. "Are you okay? When did you have her?"

"Um, she's a little more than a month old now."

"What?! But that's too early," he said, his voice breaking.

"Yeah, but she's fine. And I'm fine, too."

A single tear rolled down his cheek. I wiped it away with my fingertip.

"You... you had to do it alone? Oh, Lord. I'm sorry, Mona. I'm so sorry." He began to sob.

I squeezed his hand and fought back my own tears. "Oh, baby, I wasn't alone. My sister was with me. I had plenty of support. It wasn't like you being there, but we managed."

He covered his eyes with his hands and shook his head. I laid my hand on his head and gently rubbed his hair.

"Corey, listen," I said softly, leaning towards his ear. He wiped his eyes and looked up at me with an expression so heartbreaking that it almost pained me to look at him. "Corey," I repeated. "None of this was your fault and just because you weren't there when she was born doesn't make you any less her father."

He dropped his eyes and released a ragged sigh. "I should've been home with you. I shouldn't have left you alone so close to your due date. I just wanted to support Frederick, you know? Hey, I think he got shot, too. How is he?"

"He... he didn't make it."

"What?! Aw, man, he had a wife and kids..." He closed his eyes and shook his head. "Man..."

"I know, but the police are confident they'll catch the guy who did this."

Corey nodded and winced as he shifted in the bed.

"Are you okay? Do you need some pain medication? You want me to get a nurse?" I asked.

He shook his head. "I'm all right. That's just messed up about Frederick. He was a good guy, you know?"

I nodded. "Yeah, I know."

He sat silently for a moment and then said, "You sure the baby's okay? How are the boys?"

"She's fine, *perfect*. Cleo is watching her and Sahib back at home. The twins were here but I sent them back to school."

"What'd you name her?" he asked with a faint smile.

"I was thinking about naming her Corii with two i's instead of e-y. If that's okay with you, of course."

"After me?"

"Yeah, because I wasn't sure..." I let my voice trail off, not wanting to bring up the fact that I was afraid he wouldn't make it.

"I understand." He reached up and laced his fingers through mine. "I wanna see her."

"Well, you can see her as soon as they put you in a regular room. But in the meantime..." I pulled my cell phone from my purse. "I've got some pictures of the baby on here. We've gotta be quick because I'm not supposed to have this thing on in here."

I scrolled to a picture of Corii in Sahib's lap with Cleo holding on to her, then to a close up of Corii lying in her bassinette. A smile spread across Corey's face.

"She's beautiful." He continued to study the picture. "She's just like you."

I nodded. "Yeah, she is."

"I can't wait to see her in person."

"You will soon."

He looked at the pictures awhile longer then said, "I'm glad she's okay. But tell me, how are you, *really*?"

"I'm *really* okay."

He nodded and then closed his eyes and sighed again.

I sat down in a chair next to the bed and continued to hold his hand. We were both quiet until the nurse came in and checked on him. After she left, I broke the silence.

"Corey, do you wanna talk about what happened?"

He stared into space in silence for a full minute, and then he shook his head. "You should go back to the baby. She needs you. I'll call you later."

"Oh, okay." I stood up then leaned over and kissed him. "I'm so glad you're doing better. I love you."

He gave me a quick smile then fixed his eyes across the room on the wall. "I love you too, Mona."

I turned to leave and then hesitated. I turned back towards him. "Corey, if you decide you wanna talk about it, I'll be ready to listen."

He nodded. "I know and thank you. Kiss the baby for me."

I smiled. "I will."

I left the unit and went back to home. I was thrilled that Corey was better, but it felt like something wasn't quite right with him. I just couldn't put my finger on exactly what it was.

8

"Wrong Man"

I made as many visits to the ICU as I could over the next couple of days and was pleased with Corey's progress. The third day after his awakening, I was at the hospital bright and early so that I could see Corey for the first visitation. His mother and father were still there, of course, and his mom was actually being civil with me. I think we were all just glad Corey was awake and talking. We were glad that the worst case scenario didn't apply in this instance. There didn't seem to be any brain damage at all.

Stella even asked about the baby—finally. Maybe I had been too quick to judge her. Maybe she was just too worried about her only child to think about her new grandchild.

"She's beautiful," she said as she handed my phone back to me. "But then again, that's no surprise. I've always said you are an attractive woman. I'm sure that's how you roped my son in."

Leave it to Stella Sanders to end a compliment with a semi-insult. Before I could shoot back at her, a nurse came charging towards me. I recognized her as one of the nurses who'd been caring for Corey.

"Mrs. Sanders, please come with me. Your husband is asking, no, *demanding* to see you. He's *very* upset."

"Corey? Upset?" I asked. What in the world was going on? I looked at his parents who looked just as clueless as I felt. "O... okay."

I stood and followed the nurse into the ICU with Corey's parents on my heels. The first thing I saw when I walked into the room was Corey standing next to his bed, a wild look in his eyes. And standing at the foot of the bed was Wasif, holding a chart.

"Is what he said true, Mona?!" he shouted as soon as I entered the room.

I stood motionless, afraid to move. "W... what?"

"He's upset because I did his surgery," Wasif offered.

"Don't talk to her!" Corey roared. "Is it true, Mona?!"

"Well, yes," I answered softly.

Corey was breathing heavily as he leaned against the bed rail. "What'd you do?"

I inched towards him, a slight frown on my face. "Baby... what do you mean?"

"I mean, what the hell did you do to get him to help me?! He hates me. I *know* he didn't do it out of the goodness of his heart. WHAT DID YOU DO?!"

"I-I-I-just asked him. I *begged* him to do it."

Corey punched the mattress and looked up at me with rage in his eyes. "You are lying! What'd you do? Sleep with him? You two having an affair? *Another* affair?"

Corey's mother gasped and I heard his father whisper something to her. Then they both eased out of the room.

"Corey, listen. Nothing happened. I asked him and he agreed. That's all."

"What'd you promise him, Mona?"

"Nothing, Corey. I swear to you."

"She's telling the truth," Wasif said.

Corey glared at him. "I'm talking to my wife, *not you*. And why the hell are you still here anyway? Get out!"

"Fine," Wasif said, then he dropped Corey's chart on the bed and turned to leave. He shook his head and whispered, "I knew this was a mistake" as he walked past me.

"What?! What you say to her?" He moved towards Wasif and fell to the floor.

I dropped my purse and rushed to him. I grabbed his arm. "Corey! Are you all right? You've got to calm down!"

He snatched away from me. "Don't touch me!" he said angrily. Then his face changed and he clutched his chest. "I... I can't breathe."

"Mrs. Sanders, can you please return to the waiting area?" the nurse asked. Then she shouted, "I need some help in here!"

I stood to my feet, grabbed my purse, and slowly backed away as people crowded into Corey's room to help him. I was near tears when I walked out of the unit. I felt like I was walking through gravel as I made my way back out into the waiting room. I didn't know how to feel about what had just transpired. How was I ever going to convince him of the truth? He was so angry at me, angrier than he was when I actually did betray him. The look in his eyes was downright frightening.

I sat in the seat I had vacated only minutes earlier and hung my head. I closed my eyes and avoided looking at Corey's parents. I could only imagine the disapproving look Stella was wearing and at the moment, my fragile heart already had too many cracks in it to deal with her. Were it not for the fact that Corey was still so ill, I would've left the hospital altogether and gone home to my baby and my little boy. But angry or not, he was my husband and I loved him and he needed me whether he realized it or not.

I stayed in that waiting area through the next visit, having decided that it was best not to see him face-to-face again until he'd had time to calm down. His parents went in to see him and judging from the smirk his mother wore when they returned to the waiting area, I had been the topic of conversation during their visit. *Whatever.* I needed to know how he was, so I asked.

When they reclaimed their seats across from me, I said, "How was he?"

His mother's smirk spread into an evil little smile. "Better. They're giving him some oxygen to help with his breathing. But he's certainly upset with *you.*"

I ignored her jab. "I'm glad to hear it." I gathered my purse and stood from my seat.

"You're leaving?" Mr. Sanders asked.

"Yes, I need to get back home to my kids. I'll be back tomorrow."

"Mm-hmm, well, hopefully things will go better for you tomorrow," Stella said in a less-than-sincere tone.

"Mm-hmm," I replied as I left. I was trying. I was really trying not to cuss her out because I respected the fact that she was Corey's mother, but a saint I was not. That woman had one more time to talk crazy to me and I was going to let her have it.

***

My evil mother-in-law called me the next morning to inform me that Corey was being moved to a regular room that afternoon, so it would be best for me to wait and visit him that evening after he was all settled in. And that's what I did. Honestly, as much as I loved him and as happy as I was with his progress, I wasn't in any hurry to face him again, especially if he was still fixated on his belief that I had traded my body for his surgery.

Okay, I could see why he thought it was possible for me to do something like that, but Wasif had backed me up when I told him the truth. Wasif hated him and would've loved to see us split up, so why would he back me up? It made no sense. Couldn't Corey see that?

"What're you thinking about?" Cleo asked, shaking me from my thoughts.

I looked over at her. I'd forgotten she was sitting next to me on the sofa. I shrugged. "Everything and nothing."

"You're thinking about how Corey acted yesterday?"

I nodded. "Yeah. I just wish he'd believe me."

She rested her hand over mine. "He will. Give him some time. He's got a lot to deal with—getting shot, missing his baby's birth, finding out that his mortal enemy saved his life. Cut him some slack."

I laughed a little at the mortal enemy comment. "Mortal enemy is putting it lightly." I sighed. "I know you're right. I've just gotta support him. I'm gonna take the baby and Sahib to see him this evening. Maybe that'll keep his mind off of me and what he *thinks* I've done. All I was trying to do was save his life, Cleo. I love him so much."

"I know, Mo, and so does he. Just give him some time. The old Corey will be back before you know it."

"I hope so. In the meantime, I need to get ready to go visit *this* Corey. I can't lie and say I'm looking forward to it."

"Want me to come with you?"

"No, that's all right. I don't want to subject you to his wrath. Just help me get the kids ready."

Later that evening, I made my way through the halls of the hospital to Corey's room with a heavy heart and a cluttered mind. I silently prayed that the sight of the kids would soften his heart towards me. Upon reaching the room, I knocked lightly on the door and then opened it to find his mother and father in the room with him. His mother walked right over to me and took the baby from my arms and kissed and cooed at her like a real grandmother. Then Mr. Sanders took his turn holding her and doting on her as I slid into a chair next to Corey's bed and pulled Sahib onto my lap, but almost as soon as I sat him there, he jumped up and began to climb over the bed rail.

"Coach!" he shouted, excited to see Corey for the first time in over a month.

"No, Sahib! Get down! You're going to hurt him," I said as I reached for him.

Corey swatted my hand away. He literally *swatted* it like it was a worrisome gnat. "Leave him alone. He's fine." He raised the head of the bed and pulled Sahib onto his lap. He smiled at him as he tousled his hair. "Missed you, too, little man."

Sahib grinned and hugged Corey. Corey winced a little but I didn't say anything. I was afraid to.

"Hey, take it easy on an old man, okay?" Corey said. Sahib nodded and rested his head on Corey's chest.

Mr. Sanders handed the baby back to me and said, "Well, son, we're gonna head out and let you all visit. We're going to the hotel tonight so we can finally spend the night in a bed." He smiled at me. "Goodnight, Mona. Take care of that precious little girl."

I returned his smile. "I will."

After they left, I said, "Corey, you wanna hold her?"

He looked over at me and actually smiled. "Yes."

"Okay. Sahib, climb down and come sit with me."

Sahib obeyed and I handed Corii to her father. Corey held her in his arms and I saw his entire demeanor change. His eyes softened and his breathing slowed and, for the first time since he'd regained consciousness, he appeared to be genuinely calm and at peace.

He kissed her forehead and then he unwrapped the blanket she was swaddled in and inspected her little body, touching each finger and toe. He rubbed his hand across her hair and said, "She has hair just like you and Morgan."

I smiled. "Yes, she does. She reminds me a lot of Morgan at that age."

His expression changed. The peace was gone. "Wish I'd been around back then."

"So do I," I said quietly.

He looked up at me—his expression hardened. "Do you really?"

I nodded. "Yes. I would give anything to go back in time and have you be in Morgan's life."

He nodded and turned his attention back to the baby. "My name doesn't suit her. We should name her something else."

"Um, okay. What'd you have in mind?"

"We can name her after my mother." Was he for damn real?

"I'm sorry, I can't agree to that," I said. I didn't care how mad he was at me. I was *not* naming my child after that woman.

He frowned. "Why not?"

"Because the woman hates me or did you forget about that? If you want to name her that, we might as well name her after *my* mother."

"But you hate your mother."

"And your mother hates me. Same difference."

"She's my child, too. I have a right to name her what I want, especially since I didn't get to name my son!" he said, raising his voice.

"Damn, will I ever live that down? I didn't know he was your son, Corey. I did not keep you out of his life intentionally. He's a twin, for God's sake. I didn't even know it was possible for twins to have different fathers. I told you that!"

Sahib cringed a little in my lap. I rubbed my hand over his back and tried to calm him and myself.

"Yeah, that's what you say."

"Oh, hell, I'm leaving. There is no way I'm naming my baby after that woman. And I'm not going to sit here and let you throw the past at me. Especially not in front of my babies."

"I don't like my name for her, Mona," he said as I stood from my seat.

"Neither do I, anymore. I'll think of something else, but it sure as hell won't be Stella." I reached for the baby.

"What're you doing?" Corey asked.

"I'm leaving. Sahib is getting upset. I'm getting upset. Your blood pressure is probably up or something. I'm leaving."

"Sit down," he ordered.

I stopped and backed away from the bed a little. It wasn't what he said that made me stop. It was the tone of his voice, the look in his eyes, and his pulsating temple. I had never, *ever* seen him like that and it scared the hell out of me.

"Corey, maybe I should just go. I don't want you to have a setback," I said softly, calmly.

He stared—no, *glared* at me and said, "Are you ever going to tell me what you did? Did you sleep with him?"

I threw up my hands and sat back down as Sahib walked across the room and peered out the window. I hoped the window would keep him occupied and that he wouldn't pay Corey any attention.

"Are we back to this? Is this what the argument is really about? Corey, I was pregnant when he performed the surgery. Do you really think I slept with Wasif? And where? Here in the hospital?"

He raised an eyebrow. "You're not pregnant anymore."

"I just had a baby. I'm not trying to have sex with anyone right now. Not even you!"

"So you're saying he did this without getting anything in return?"

"Yes, Corey. That's *exactly* what I'm saying! I know you hate him and I know he can be manipulative at times, but he's not some heartless monster. He did it because I asked him to do it and yes, because he cares about me. But I offered him nothing in return except for my gratitude. That is the God's honest truth!"

"Nia," he said.

I frowned and gripped my throbbing head. "What?"

"That was one of the names you mentioned awhile back. Nia—after Nia Long. I like it. She looks like a Nia."

What the hell? "So we're done discussing Wasif and we're back to naming the baby?"

"Yeah. Nia's good. What do you think for a middle name?"

I sat there for a moment and looked at him. He looked calm, like we hadn't just argued—like he hadn't transformed from Dr. David Banner into the Incredible Hulk just minutes earlier.

"Well?" he insisted.

"Um... if we're going with actress names, then Gabrielle would be good. I-I like Gabrielle Union, too."

He smiled as he looked down at the baby. "Nia Gabrielle Sanders. It fits. We'll go with that."

I nodded. "Okay."

We sat there in silence for a while. Sahib stayed at the window for a little longer and then climbed back onto my lap and rubbed his eyes.

"Looks like our little man is sleepy. You better go on home. See you tomorrow?" Corey asked.

I stood and took the baby from him. "Yeah, sure." I moved to back away from him but he grabbed my arm and, almost instantly, my heart began to race.

"Hey," he said. "Come here."

I clutched the baby to my chest and leaned closer to Corey. He reached up and kissed me softly then he smiled and said, "I love you."

"I... I love you, too."

As I turned to leave, he gently swatted my bottom. "Man, I can't wait to get back home to you."

I smiled stiffly and took my kids and got out of that room. There was only one thought running through my mind as I made my way out to my car: *What the hell is wrong with my husband?*

9

"Body And Soul"

"He's out of his mind, Cleo, and don't say I'm just overreacting. The doctors were wrong. He *does* have brain damage. He's freakin' schizophrenic now," I said as I sat at the kitchen table and watched my sister cook.

"Okay, maybe he's having a few mood swings right now. Like I said, give him some time. I mean, he did come back to himself eventually, right?" she said as she flipped a pork chop in the skillet.

"Yeah, but the whole thing was just eerie. I mean, Corey and I have always understood our roles in this marriage. *I'm* the crazy one, Cleo—not *him*. What in the world are we going to do if both of us are loony? We can't raise kids like that."

She shrugged. "Well, I guess you're just gonna have to stop being crazy then." She turned and gave me a sly grin.

"Ha, ha, ha," I said dryly. "You know what I mean. I'm just saying, what if this is permanent? What if all I have to look forward to in the future is him mood-swinging all over the place? How am I gonna cope with that?"

She sat down across from me at the table. "From what you told me, the source of his rage was Wasif. Once he gets over Wasif doing the surgery, I'm sure things will be fine."

I sighed. "Lord knows I hope you're right. I'm ashamed to say this, but for a moment there, I was beginning to think that maybe I shouldn't have worked so hard to get him back, that maybe I should've just moved on with Wasif."

Cleo frowned and leaned forward, her eyes glued to me. "Now you listen to me. That kind of thinking will get you in a lot of trouble. You love him—I know it, you know it, and Corey knows it. You almost lost him and nearly lost your mind because of it. He can't help what happened to him and it's understandable that his emotions would be erratic right now. Don't you go making a bad situation worse by messing with Wasif. Messing with him is like playing with fire and I can guarantee you'll get burned. And you *will* lose Corey forever."

I let her words sink in and said, "You're right. I know you're right. I told you I was crazy."

"And I told you to stop being crazy."

I heard the faint ringing of my cell phone. "Shoot, I left it in the bedroom. I better get it before it wakes the baby up."

Cleo stood from her chair. "No, I'll get it. Just watch the food for me."

A few seconds later, she returned to the kitchen with my phone and said, "Speak of the devil and he will appear."

I took the phone and saw that the call had come from Wasif. I rolled my eyes. "Let me call him back."

I dialed his number and he answered after the first ring.

"Hey," I said. "You called?"

"Yeah, look, I know I was supposed to pick Sahib up this evening but I'm gonna be stuck here at the hospital for a while. Are you coming to visit Sanders? If so, can you bring Sahib to me?"

"Oh, sure. No problem."

"Great. Just call me when you get here. He can make rounds with me."

I smiled. "I'm sure he'll like that."

"All right, well, see you then."

"Okay." I hung up and when I looked up, Cleo was staring at me.

"What?" I said.

"That's what I wanna know," she replied.

"He just wants me to bring Sahib to the hospital instead of him coming here to get him."

"That's probably better. You gonna tell Corey?"

"I don't have to run my every move by Corey. Besides, the last thing I want to do is bring Wasif's name up to him."

"I'm telling you, you better tell him. It'd be your luck for his mom to see you with Wasif. I bet she'd gladly spill the beans to him."

I released a frustrated sigh, picked up my phone, and called Corey's room. "You don't always have to be right and make sense and stuff, you know?" I said to Cleo as the phone rang in my ear.

She smiled and shrugged.

"Hello," Corey finally answered in a groggy voice.

"Hey, Corey. Did I wake you?"

"Yeah, but you're allowed to. How you doing, baby? What's up?" He sounded so good and sweet and sexy, I nearly melted.

"Hey, I'm gonna take Sahib to Wasif at the hospital before heading on up to see you this evening. I just wanted you to know."

"Okay, baby. That's fine. I can't wait to see you. I miss you. Love you."

I smiled. "I think I love you just a little bit more."

"We'll just see about that. Bye, baby."

This time Cleo was smiling at me when I ended the call. "Sounds like I was right again."

"Yeah, he sounded like his old self. Shoot, I think he actually sounded a little *better* than his old self."

"Good. Let's get Sahib to the table and start eating dinner. I swear he reminds me of myself, always in front of a TV."

"He sure is. Thanks, again, Cleo. *For everything*. Hopefully, Corey will get to come home soon and you can go back home to Scott and the kids."

"No rush. Like I said, I'm here for as long as you need me. I hope you'll come visit after I get back home."

"We will once everything calms down. You still gotta teach me how to ride a horse."

"Yeah, because that was a disaster last time," she said through a chuckle.

"Look, I had no idea horses were so big. Randy freaked me out."

She laughed harder. "*Mandy* was just a pony."

"Mandy, Randy, Candy... whatever. He scared me to death,"

More laughter. "*She!*"

"Yeah, yeah, yeah. Go ahead and laugh at me."

"I'm sorry, big sis, but that was *hilarious*."

"If I didn't need you right now, I swear…"

"Whatever, girl. Let's eat."

***

Wasif met me in the parking lot, greeting both Sahib and me with a smile. "Thanks for bringing him to me," he said.

"Not a problem. See you Sunday evening." I bent over and kissed Sahib's cheek. "Be a good boy for your dad."

Wasif grasped Sahib's hand. "He's always a good boy. Everything okay with you?" He peered over into the baby carrier. "She's beautiful, Mo. I always wondered what our daughter would look like. Never got the chance to find out."

I felt a little ill at ease, as if Corey could hear him or something. "Well, you have two daughters and two sons. I'm sure that's more than enough for you with you having to juggle visitation and everything."

"*Three* sons," he said with raised eyebrows.

"Yes, that's what I meant. Well, let me get inside the building. It's too windy out here for the baby."

"Of course. Sorry for keeping you out here. Bye."

"Bye."

I watched as he and Sahib walked towards the hospital's employee entrance and then I began to walk to the front door. I had nearly made it into the hospital when a familiar voice stopped me in my tracks.

"Why didn't you just go with him?" It was Corey whom I hadn't noticed sitting in a wheelchair near the entrance.

"Hey! What are you doing out here?" I asked, purposely ignoring his question.

"My wife said she was bringing my daughter to see me and I just couldn't wait, so I decided to sit out here and watch them arrive. And what did I see? My wife staring at her lover."

I sighed. "He's not my lover, Corey. Don't do this, okay? Let's just go back up to your room."

He stared at me for a long minute and then looked at the baby carrier. "Yeah, let's get the baby out of this air. Let me hold her. You can push me."

I handed him the carrier and we headed up to his room with no further discussion of me or Wasif, thank goodness. Once we arrived at his room, I helped him into bed and then took Nia out of the carrier and handed her to him. "Where're your parents?" I asked.

He kept his eyes on the baby as he spoke. "They were here earlier. They went back to their hotel."

I nodded and sat there in silence as he smiled and whispered to the baby. I had all of my fingers and toes crossed that he wouldn't bring Wasif up again. The nurse came in and checked him and a few minutes after she left, Corey said, "The baby's sleep. You wanna put her back in the carrier?"

"Yeah, sure." I took the baby and placed her in the carrier on the floor and then reclaimed my seat. Corey smiled over at me as he looked me up and down. "You look good, baby."

I blushed a little. "Thank you."

"Come here."

I stood and walked over to the bed and he grasped my hand and pulled me into a kiss like none I'd ever received from him before. Once the kiss had ended, he said, "You wanna do something?"

I frowned slightly. "Here?"

He smiled. "Yeah, baby. Where else?" He pulled me into another kiss.

"We might get caught."

"We won't. I can set my watch by these nurses. No one will be back for another couple of hours."

"But you're still not well."

"I'm well enough to do this."

"But the baby is only five weeks old. The doctor won't release me for another week."

"That didn't stop us after Sahib was born."

"But, Corey…"

His eyes narrowed. "I'm your husband and you're standing here making up excuses not to have sex with me. You used to love it."

"I *still* love it. I just don't think it's a good idea to do it here… and now."

I backed away a little and he grasped my wrist tightly. "You saving it for someone else?"

"Huh? What? Well, yeah. I'm saving it for *you*."

He leaned in and kissed my neck. "So it's mine, right?"

"You know it is."

"Then stop arguing with me and climb up in this bed." He kissed me again.

Okay, it had been a while and all of that kissing wasn't helping matters, and he was my husband and I missed his touch, so... I climbed into that bed with him.

***

My legs were wobbly as I slowly made my way from Corey's room to my car. If what had just happened in that room was a side-effect of him being shot, then let me say that if it weren't for the fact that he almost died, I kind of wished he'd been shot a long time ago. He was on fire! I mean hot lava-type fire. I could've stayed in that room all night if it meant I could have some more of that.

As I slid into my car, my cell phone rang. "Hello?" I answered.

"Hey, baby? You on your way home?" It was Corey.

"Yes, but I miss you already."

"Really? So you liked that?"

"You know I did. Did you?"

"Well, I'm sitting here back on oxygen, so I guess I liked it too much."

I tightly gripped the steering wheel. "Oxygen! I knew it was too soon!"

"No, baby. I'm fine. It's just that my lung is still healing. I'm good, better since we did what we did."

"But you're on oxygen again!"

"I'm fine. See you tomorrow?"

"Yes, of course."

"We can go for round two."

"Corey…"

"Don't fuss. Just say goodnight."

I sighed. "Goodnight."

We ended the call and I drove home with no intentions of telling anyone, including my sister, that I'd just sexed my husband in his hospital room.

10

"I Can't Sleep"

A few days later, I was helping Corey get ready to go home when he hit me with the news.

"Mama and Daddy are gonna stay with us for a couple of weeks."

I stopped in the middle of zipping up the duffel bag. "Stay with us where?"

"At our house. Where else?"

"What's wrong with the hotel room?"

"Baby, I can't let them keep staying in a hotel when we have that big, new house to share. Besides, can you imagine the money they've spent so far?"

"I'm sure they have it to spend."

"Come on, Mona. They just want to help. I mean, we've got the baby and I'm still not 100%. I've got physical therapy and doctor's visits. We need the help."

"My sister can help."

"I thought you sent her home yesterday."

"She'll come back if I ask her to."

"Didn't you say you felt bad about her being away from her family?"

"Not as bad as I'll feel about cussing your mother out."

"You're not going to cuss my mother out."

I dropped the bag on the floor and sat in the chair next to his bed. "I'm glad you think so. But I'm not so confident in my level of self-control, especially if she says something crazy to me."

"She won't. Come on, she's my mother—not Satan."

I folded my arms at my chest. "No comment."

"Come here."

I shook my head. "No."

"Come on, baby. Come here."

I sighed, stood from the chair, and walked over to the bed. He continued holding the baby in one arm and reached for me with the other. He kissed me and smiled. "I promise it'll be okay."

"Corey, we're talking about me and your mother sleeping under the same roof. This is going to be a disaster."

"No-it-won't," he said, separating each word with a soft kiss.

"Okay, *I guess.* But don't think you can keep seducing me into agreeing with you. It ain't gonna work forever."

He grinned as he gave me a peck on the cheek. "I'm not seducing you. If I was seducing you, you'd already be out of those clothes."

I blushed and as he kissed me once again, there was a knock at his door. Our lips were still locked when the door opened to reveal his parents, who hadn't bothered to wait for us to answer it.

We parted and Corey said, "Hey, you two. Ready to come bunk with us?"

"As ready as we'll ever be," Stella said, sounding about as enthusiastic as I felt.

"Great! We're so happy you'll be staying with us. Isn't that right, baby?" he said with a big grin on his face.

I gritted my teeth, gave Cruella Stella a fake smile, and said, "Sure." I turned back to Corey. "Let me take this bag downstairs and pull the car around. I'll be right back."

He nodded and kissed me. "Okay, baby. Hurry."

As I made my way to the door, Stella said, "My goodness! You two act like a couple of newlyweds." And she sounded like she was truly appalled.

"I *feel* like a newlywed, Mama. I'm alive, I've got a new baby, and I about to go home to my gorgeous wife."

I smiled and ducked out of the room before she could respond.

We made it home and were so busy getting settled in that first night that I didn't have time to think about Stella and she didn't have a chance to get on my nerves. Thanksgiving was in a week, and the twins would be home. Hopefully there would be enough people in my house to make me forget she was even there.

When we climbed into bed that night, Corey's libido was in overdrive again, but I definitely didn't mind. When we finally fell asleep, I was more than exhausted, but it was a good exhaustion. It was a my-husband-is-home-and-alive-and-better-than-ever exhaustion.

My much needed sleep was interrupted early the next morning, but not by Nia's cries as I was accustomed to. It was Corey thrashing around in the bed that was to blame. I sat up and turned a lamp on. Corey was drenched in sweat, sitting up in the bed with a look of terror on his face. I reached for him but he snatched away and looked over at me. He stared at me for a moment, his expression changing from fear, to confusion, to recognition. Without a word, he stood from the bed and stumbled to the bathroom, slamming the door behind him.

I walked over to the door and placed my hands on it. "Corey… Corey, are you okay?"

No answer from inside the bathroom.

I looked over at the bassinette, where Nia was still fast asleep, and then I turned my attention back to the door. "Corey, baby, are you okay in there?"

Silence.

"Baby, please say something."

"Go… go back to bed, Mona."

"Are you okay?"

"Yeah, just go back to bed. *Please*, go back to bed. Okay?"

"O… okay."

"And turn the light back off."

"All right. Hurry back to bed."

I climbed back into bed, turned the lamp off, and stared into the darkness. I rested my hand on Corey's side of the bed and felt wetness. His sweat had drenched the sheets. I lay there for a moment and then decided that since I couldn't sleep and Corey didn't seem to be coming out of that bathroom anytime soon, I would change the sheets. As I stripped the bed, I got a whiff of something that stopped me in my tracks. There was more than sweat on those sheets. It was urine I smelled. Corey had wet the bed.

***

The next morning, Corey slept late and I didn't bother him because I honestly didn't know what to say to him. So the best thing I could think to do was to get up and cook him a huge breakfast of the things he loved. That plan was derailed when I walked into the kitchen to find Stella's bony behind turned up. She was bent over, looking in the refrigerator. I stood and stared at her and resisted the urge to kick her into the refrigerator and shut the door.

She finally stood up and turned around with an arm full of food. She didn't notice me standing in the doorway as she walked across the kitchen dropped the food into the trash can.

I frowned, stepped forward, and made myself known. "What are you doing?"

She looked up at me and then walked back over to the refrigerator. "Oh, didn't hear you come in. I'm cleaning out the refrigerator. I'm sure you haven't had time to do it."

I had no idea what she could've been cleaning out of the refrigerator since Cleo had already cleaned it out for me. I made my way over to the trash can and peered inside. Sure enough, she'd thrown away perfectly good food.

"Um, I just bought this food the other day. It's still good," I said, pointing at the trash can.

She walked over to me. "Oh, I didn't say the food wasn't good, just not good for Corey or the kids, or you for that matter. I mean, those hips of yours are getting pretty wide."

My mouth fell open. Was this woman for real? "Okay, let me make some things clear to you. This is *my* home, Stella. I am the lady of this house. I buy whatever I want to buy and I feed my family whatever I want to feed them. And you should know that Corey has never complained about what I feed him and he damn sure hasn't complained about my hips."

She smiled and tilted her head to the side. "What is it?"

I crossed my arms over my chest and squared my shoulders. "What is *what*?"

"What is it about you that he sees? I mean, when I look at you, all I see is a chubby, uneducated, harlot. Are you *that* good in bed?"

I returned her smile and stepped closer to her. "I'm better than you think."

She shook her head. "I trusted you with my son. I let you into my home. I gave you the benefit of the doubt even though I knew you were nothing more than a low-class pretty face. And what did you do? You broke my boy's heart."

I laughed wryly. "Man, I heard that old people get stuck in the past. I guess you've proven that theory right. Standing here bringing up ancient-damn-history. You are sad. Get some new material."

She stepped a little closer to me. "You better watch your mouth."

I twisted my neck and raised an eyebrow. "Or what? Just because I've been holding my tongue around you and trying to keep the peace doesn't mean I'm weak. You put a finger on me and I'ma put you down. You better believe that!"

"I will never understand what my son sees in you. You are nothing more than common street trash!"

I smiled. "Hmm, well, I can tell you this: your son *loves* him some street trash. *Can't get enough of it.* Now, if you hate me so much, you are more than welcome to leave. But for now, get the hell out of my kitchen so I can cook my *husband* some breakfast."

"What's going on in here?" Corey asked, breaking up our little confrontation. He was standing just inside the kitchen with Nia in his arms.

I looked over at Stella and gave her a slight shake of my head. She frowned a little but evidently she got the message.

"Um… nothing. I think Mona was just about to cook you some breakfast. And I was wondering if this little lady was awake." She walked over to Corey, kissed him on the cheek, and took Nia from him. "You okay, Corey?" she asked.

"I'm fine, Mama."

Stella left the kitchen and I walked over to Corey and hugged him. "You sure you're okay?" I asked.

He rested his hand on my back. "Yeah, I'm good, baby."

"You wanna talk—"

He pulled away from me. "I said I was good. What's for breakfast?"

I walked over to the refrigerator and peered inside. "Well, we're out of bacon, but I can make some steak and eggs if you want."

"Sounds good. I'm gonna go watch TV with my dad."

I nodded. "Okay."

I was in the middle of cooking when his mother returned to the kitchen. "What's going on?" she asked.

Without looking up from the stove, I said, "What are you talking about?"

"Why didn't you tell Corey about the argument? I would think you'd be glad to try to make me look bad in his eyes."

I turned to face her. "Look, he didn't have a good night last night. I didn't see the point in upsetting him."

She gave me a shocked look. "Really?"

"Wow, you act like I'm the devil or something."

She raised her eyebrows. "Well…"

I sighed. "Whatever. Can you please leave now?"

She glanced over at the stove. "Red meat? You're going to kill my son."

As she left the kitchen, I whispered, "Witch."

11

"Men In My Life"

"Stop laughing! None of this is funny, Cleo. I swear I'ma cuss this woman out!" I said.

"Okay, okay. Calm down. She's just trying to get under your skin," Cleo replied.

"Well, she's succeeding. I mean, first she throws my doggone food away, and then she insults me for cooking red meat. *Then* she has the nerve to complain about it being well-done. Talking about I cooked all of the nutrients out. I told her I cooked it the way Corey likes it and I shoulda told her to look at her own husband. The man was eating so fast I was afraid he'd choke! Anyway, after that little statement, she got her bony butt up and fixed herself a smoothie. *I can't stand her!*"

Cleo laughed into the phone again. "It's only been a couple of days, Mo. And she's just trying to be health conscious."

"Well, if she keeps messing with me, she might become conscious of my foot up her tail."

More laughter. "Where are you now?"

"In the car, on the parking lot of the grocery store."

"You replacing the food she threw away?"

"Yeah, I'ma go in there and buy all of the pork and beef I can get my hands on. I hope she has a freakin' stroke when she sees it."

"What are you gonna do if she throws it away again?"

"Girl, they gon' have to call the police to peel me off of her. Anyway, let me get in this store so I can get back home to my kids. She's probably spiked Nia's bottle with some wheat germ by now."

"You're crazy. I'll talk to you later."

"I'm not crazy, girl, I'm serious. The rate things are going, I might be knocking on your door soon looking for some political asylum."

"Lord, help you. Bye, Mo."

"Bye."

I climbed out of my car and made my way through the grocery store, glad to be alone for a moment. I had a lot on my mind— Corey, his parents' constant presence, and Wasif's engagement. I know I shouldn't have cared, but I did. It was kind of a hard pill for me to swallow—him moving on with his life. Him with another woman. Him *marrying* another woman—again.

In the back of my mind, I wondered what had happened to his big declaration of love to me. What happened to the whole, "I don't want anyone but you" speech? Was he lying? Just saying what he thought I wanted to hear in order to get me to change my mind? Evidently so. I tried to shake the thoughts from my head. After all, I had other issues to deal with.

I hadn't told Cleo about the incident with Corey wetting the bed, having decided that some things were meant only for me and him to know about. But I was worried about him. The second night he was home, he'd tossed and turned all night. I don't think he slept more than five minutes the whole night and I slept even less than that. I could hear him mumbling in his sleep, but couldn't make out the words. I wanted to help him, but he just kept right on with the lie about him being fine.

I rounded the corner, heading to the produce aisle and nearly ran right into a petite little blonde woman. "Oh, sorry!" I said. "Excuse me."

"It's okay," she said with a bright smile.

I smiled and as I passed her, I heard someone call my name. I turned around to see Wasif standing there with his arm around the blonde woman's shoulder. What the hell?

"Wasif?" I said with a slight frown.

He smiled. "Ann, this is Mo, my ex. Mo, this is my fiancée, Ann."

I offered the best smile I could, because I was honestly shocked. Wasif was with *her*? I just didn't see how that was going to work out. All of the things Wasif always liked about me—wide hips and an ample backside—this woman did not possess.

"Hi," I managed to say.

"Hi!" she replied a little too enthusiastically, "I am so glad to finally meet you. I just love little Sahib and I'm looking forward to getting to know the twins better. They are all so handsome!"

"Well, thank you. I'm proud of them."

"You should be! Oh, Wasif, sweetie, I forgot the strawberries. Be right back." She kissed him on the cheek and scurried away.

I smiled at him. "Wow."

He frowned a little. "Wow, what?"

"Oh, nothing. She just wasn't what I expected."

"Really?"

"Yeah, really. But she's nice, so best of luck to you."

"Um, thanks. How are you? How's the new baby?"

"We're good. Don't forget you get Sahib next weekend."

"I won't."

We stood there in silence for a second, then Wasif said, "I miss you, Mo."

And before I could stop my fool self, I replied with, "I miss you, too."

Thank God and all of the heavenly hosts that Ann returned before we started stripping right there in the middle of the store because, knowing me and Wasif and the attraction we'd always shared, that was a real possibility. I said a quick goodbye and rushed through the rest of my shopping. I was almost relieved to return to my circus of a home because I really didn't want to head back down the road of troubles that opening the door on a relationship with Wasif would lead to.

I carried the bags into the kitchen and was busy putting the food up when Corey startled me.

"Where the hell you been?" he asked in a menacing voice.

The only thing obstructing my view of his face was the freezer door and I was afraid to shut it. So I kept it open, allowing the cold air to cover my face. "I was at the grocery store. Remember?"

"What took so long?"

"There was a line at the checkout," I lied. But that sounded better than "I was in the car talking about your mama to Cleo and then I ran into Wasif and told him I missed him."

"Must've been pretty damn long."

"It was."

He walked over to me and grabbed my arm. He pulled me backwards and shut the freezer door. Then he stared into my eyes and repeated his question. "Where were you, Mona-Lisa?"

With a furrowed brow, I said, "I told you. I was at the store. Where do you think I was?"

He tightened his grasp on my arm and pulled me from the kitchen, through the living room, to our bedroom. He slammed the bedroom door behind us. Then he began to kiss me and undress me at the same time.

When he finally removed his mouth from mine, I said, "What are you doing?"

"What does it look like?" he asked as he kissed my neck.

"Where are Sahib and Nia?"

"With my parents, in the den."

"What if they hear us?"

He lifted his head. "You don't want me or something, Mona?"

"No, no, it's not that, but it's the middle of the day and your parents are here and—"

He backed away from me. "You were with *him*, weren't you?"

"With who?" I asked, as if I didn't know who he was referring to.

"Who? Who else, Mona? The same *who* it always is!"

"No! I just went to the store!"

"What? Is it time for you to pay him back for doing the surgery?"

I walked over to the bed and slumped onto it. "Not *this* again. I did not promise him anything, Corey. I am not sleeping with him. I love you and only you. I only want *you*."

He walked over to me and brushed his hand over my hair. "Then stop stalling."

"Is this what things are gonna be like, Corey? Am I gonna have to have sex with you every time you think I've been with Wasif? You are being paranoid and ridiculous!"

"So something's wrong with *me*? You can't keep your legs closed when you're around him and you know it! I don't know why I'm still with you, anyway!"

I looked up at him for a second and realized that what he'd just said had been in his mind for much longer than that moment. I stood from the bed and looked him in the eye. "So that's how you really feel, huh?"

He frowned and a confused look crossed his face. "No, no, I don't."

"Yeah, you do. You just finally got angry enough to say it."

He grabbed me and pulled me to him. I didn't hug him back. "I'm sorry, baby. I didn't mean to say that. I love you, Mona. I'm sorry."

"Let go of me, Corey."

He complied and I walked over to the door and opened it. "Are you leaving?" he asked softly, his voice breaking.

I turned and looked at him. "I'm just going to check on my children."

He slowly moved toward me. "Wait, baby. Don't go. I just need you. I need to feel you and be close to you. *I'm sorry.*"

I shook my head. "Corey, you can't—"

Before I could finish my statement, Corey grabbed me and held me so tightly I could barely breathe.

"I'm scared, baby. I'm so scared," he whispered into my ear. "I'm scared I'm gonna lose you."

"Corey, look at me," I said as I tried to loosen his grip.

"Baby, please don't leave me."

"Corey… Corey, look at me."

He backed away a little, his arms still around me. He looked at me with eyes that reminded me of Sahib's when he heard thunder or saw lightening.

"Corey, I love you. I choose you and only you. I don't want anyone else. *I love you.*"

"I'm messed up, baby. I can't take care of you *or* protect you." He rubbed his hand across his chest. "This… it messed me up, Mona. It really messed me up."

"Then talk to me, baby. Tell me about it. *Please.*"

"I can't. I don't want to think about it anymore."

"It's not just gonna go away. I tried that method, remember? You've gotta talk to someone. A counselor, maybe?"

He shook his head and backed away from me. "No, I just need you. Just stay with me, okay? We don't have to do anything, I just need to hold you, okay? Will you just let me do that?"

I nodded. "Okay."

We both climbed into the bed and I wrapped my arms around my husband. He laid his head on my chest and soon drifted off to sleep as I caressed his back and kissed his forehead. And as I began to drift off myself, I prayed that God would show me how to help him.

12

"Just Because"

Things were rolling along okay until the day of Corey's first physical therapy session. I could sense his anxiety when he was getting dressed, but I didn't say anything. I just laid out his clothes and cooked his breakfast and tried to be supportive in those ways. His mother and father drove him to his session and I stayed behind with the kids and cleaned my home and cooked lunch and waited for him to return.

I was sitting in the den watching TV with Sahib while feeding Nia when I heard the front door open. Corey's parents entered the den with harried looks on their faces and then I heard a door slam in my house. I looked over at his parents who just stood in the middle of the floor in silence.

"Didn't go well?" I asked.

"Not at all," his father said quietly.

His mother just shook her head and left the den without a word.

I stood from my seat and balanced Nia on my hip. "Sahib, stay put. I'll be right back."

"Yes, ma'am," he said without turning his attention away from the TV.

"I'll keep an eye on him," Mr. Sanders said.

"Thanks," I replied and then made my way from the den to my

bedroom, where I was sure Corey was holed up.

Sure enough, my bedroom door was shut and locked. I knocked lightly on it. "Corey?"

No answer.

"Corey, it's Mona. Can you let me in?"

Silence.

"Baby, please let me in."

I heard the lock click on the door, but it didn't open. I turned the knob, slowly opened the door, and walked inside to find Corey sitting on the side of the bed with his head hung low. I stood there for a few seconds before sitting down next to him. I held Nia to my chest and rested my hand on his thigh. He looked over at me, defeat in his eyes. Then he stood from the bed and I got a good look at him. He was still my husband. He was still handsome and tall and, though he'd lost some weight and some of his bulk, he was *still* fine.

He was still Corey, but a part of him—the smile in his eyes, the quiet strength he'd always exhibited—those things were missing. Gone were the confidence and the power that I'd always been so attracted to. Standing before me was a shell of the man I knew and loved so much and to see him like that disturbed me.

"What happened today?" I asked. "During therapy, did something happen to upset you?"

He nodded and began to rub the back of his neck with his hand. He backed into the door and leaned against it. "They had me doing this simple stuff, you know? Walking, lifting these tiny weights, and I got out of breath. I couldn't finish anything."

"Well, you were shot in the lung. It's just going to take some time for you to fully recover, baby. It'll get better."

"But what if it doesn't? How the hell am I gonna run a fitness center when I can't walk an inch without getting short of breath? I'm losing my form. I look a damn mess. How am I gonna live like this, Mona?"

I stood from the bed and walked over to him. I laid my hand on his arm. "You still look mighty fine to me, Coach Sanders."

He gave me a small smile. "Yeah, right. You're supposed to say that."

"Look, it doesn't matter to me if you get scrawny like you were in college, I'ma still love you and I'm staying right by your side. You've got to stop being so hard on yourself, baby. Just give yourself and your body some time, okay?" I kissed his cheek.

He lifted his head and kissed me softly on the lips. "I don't know what I'd do if I didn't have you, Mona-Lisa."

"Lucky for you, you'll never have to find out."

***

As the days passed, things got better for Corey. He even started sleeping more at night. It was the week of Thanksgiving, his parents' last week with us, and the twins were home to visit. Nia was growing like a healthy little weed. Sahib was still just as sweet and smart as ever. I hadn't had anymore confessional run-ins with Wasif. I'd have to say that things were better than better at that point. They were actually rather great.

I was busy prepping for Thanksgiving dinner with my baby in her little carrier staring at me and Sahib somewhat helping me pick greens. Corey and Blair were in the den watching a ball game with

Corey's father and Stella was somewhere around the house. I didn't care where as long as she wasn't bothering me. Morgan was out with some of his friends. Things were quiet and peaceful and I should've known that meant trouble was brewing somewhere.

The first indication that the bottom was about to fall out of my life was a knock at the front door. We weren't expecting anyone and Morgan had a key. The second indication was Corey yelling my name.

I grabbed my two babies and rushed to the front door to see one of our gym clients standing in the doorway with his hand on Morgan's arm. Did I mention that the client was a police officer?

"What's going on?" I asked.

"Mark did us a favor by bringing Morgan home instead of arresting him," Corey said, his eyes glued to Morgan.

"Arresting him for what?" I asked.

"Trying to buy a gun off the street. Just so happened he tried to buy it from an undercover cop. When Mark got wind of it, he stepped in and brought Morgan home."

"Morgan! What in the world is wrong with you?! Why would you be trying to buy a gun?"

Morgan shrugged, his eyes trained on his own feet. "I needed one."

"Needed one for what?! Is something going on at school? Is there something you need to tell us?"

"Hold on, Mona. Let me walk Mark out," Corey said. "Thanks, again, man."

"Hey, no problem. I know y'all are good people. Hate to see

anything tragic happen," Mark replied.

As Corey walked Mark out, I stood and stared at my son and wondered what in hell was on his mind trying to buy a gun. I had to bite my tongue to wait until Corey returned, but as soon as he walked back in, I lit into Morgan.

"Tell me what the hell is going on, Morgan! Why do you need a gun?"

He shrugged. "Because."

"Boy, I don't care how old you are, I will snatch a knot in you if you don't tell me what's going on!" I shouted. Seconds later, Blair had joined us in the foyer.

"I don't want to talk about it," he said.

I moved closer to him. "Morgan, the police just brought you home. You owe us an explanation and you need to start talking *now*."

"I need it to take care of some business."

"Boy, what business you got that requires a damn gun?" I said as Mr. Sanders stepped up behind me.

Morgan sighed as if I was getting on his nerves or something. "It's personal."

"Personal? Personal?! The moment your tail almost got arrested and had to be escorted home by the police, *personal* flew out the window!" I shouted.

Corey's eyes canvased the small crowd that had formed in the foyer of our home. "Um, let's take this to our bedroom, Mona," he said.

I almost screamed at him, and then I caught myself. He was right. There was no need in us putting on a show for his parents and all of the yelling was probably scaring Sahib and Nia.

I nodded slightly and said, "Okay."

We excused ourselves and Corey grabbed Morgan's arm and steered him to our bedroom where he leaned against the closed door and folded his arms over his chest. I took a seat on the edge of my bed next to Corey.

"Now, you wanna tell us what's going on?" Corey asked.

"I already told you. I needed a gun."

"For what, Morgan? Why would you *need* one?" I asked.

Morgan didn't reply.

"Boy, you hear your mama. Answer her!" Corey bellowed. A vein in his temple bulged. If he didn't intimidate Morgan, he sure scared the hell out of me.

Morgan looked up at Corey. "I need a gun so I can do what the police won't do."

"What's that? What are you talking about, Morgan?" I asked.

He squared his shoulders and straightened his posture. "I know who shot Coach, Mama! Everybody knows it! The police know it, and they ain't trying to arrest him! So, if they won't take care of it, I will."

"Morgan, the police are doing what they can. You can't just go out and buy a gun and shoot someone on-sight because you feel like it," I said and then glanced over at Corey. He was silent, his eyes fixed on something across the room.

"I gotta do something, Mama! Dude tried to kill my father! I can't just sit around like a chump and let him get away with it!"

I heard Morgan, but I couldn't take my eyes off of Corey. He looked like he'd totally zoned out, like he was no longer a part of the conversation.

I shifted my eyes from Corey to Morgan. Morgan saw it, too. "Coach, you okay?" he asked.

Silence from Corey.

"D... Dad, you all right?" he repeated.

I rested my hand on Corey's arm. He snatched away from me and jumped up from the bed, a wild look in his eyes. "Get back," he said.

I frowned. "Corey... Corey, what's wrong?"

He looked over at me as if just realizing who I was. "What?" he asked.

"Are you okay, Dad?" Morgan asked again.

Corey smiled a little and reclaimed his seat on the bed. "You called me 'Dad.'"

Morgan nodded. "Yeah, that's what you are, right?"

Corey nodded. "Yeah."

Morgan sighed as he walked over and squeezed in between me and Corey on the bed. "I'm sorry, Dad. I just... I can't stand the fact that that dude hurt you and he's getting away with it."

Corey wrapped his arm around Morgan's shoulder. "He's not getting away with it, son. If the police don't get him, God will take care of it. I'm certain of that."

"Yes, sir."

"No more trying to buy guns, okay? We raised you better than that. If you get in that kind of trouble, it'll kill your mother and I don't know how well I'll be able to deal with it, either."

Morgan nodded. "Yes, sir. I'm sorry."

Corey smiled at Morgan. "All right. I'll talk to you some more later on. I get tired so much easier now. I think I'ma go to bed."

"Yes, sir."

After Morgan left the room, I sat on the edge of the bed with Nia on my lap and watched as Corey walked into the bathroom and brushed his teeth. When he returned to our room and started to shed his clothes, I said, "You okay?"

He looked up at me and offered me a little smile. "I'm fine." He pulled on a pair of pajama bottoms and then walked over to me and took Nia from my arms.

"Are you sure? You seemed to kind of zone out a little earlier when we were talking to Morgan."

He sat down beside me, kissed Nia's forehead, and said, "I did?"

"Yes."

"Oh, I don't know what happened then, but I'm fine now. Ready for bed. Are *you* okay?"

"Yeah, I'm good. Just worried about Morgan... and you."

"I think we got through to Morgan, and I'ma talk to him again tomorrow. And don't worry about me. I'm good, baby. I'll show you just how good I am once little mama goes to sleep." He leaned over and kissed me softly.

"Oh, really?"

He smiled. "Really."

"Well, let me go get her a bottle so we can get this started."

"Yeah, you go do that, because I got something for you. Shoot, when I get through with you, *you* might be the one on oxygen."

He wasn't playing, either. When he was done with me later on that night, I could've sworn I was having an asthma attack—and I don't have asthma.

13

"Plenty Of Room"

Thanksgiving morning, I woke up bright and early and headed to the kitchen to make breakfast while my family slept. I was nearly done cooking when I was joined in the kitchen by Morgan.

"Good morning, Mama," he said as he took a seat at the table. The older he got, the more he looked like Corey. Since starting college, he'd even begun lifting weights, giving him muscles that rivaled his father's.

"Good morning. Sleep well?" I replied.

"No, actually, I didn't."

I stopped what I was doing and joined him at the table. "Why? What's the matter?"

"I'm worried about Coach. You see how be blanked out last night?"

"Yeah, I noticed that."

"Does he do that a lot?"

I sighed and weighed in my mind just how much about Corey's condition I should share with Morgan. Morgan was almost twenty years old, an adult, and Corey was his father. I decided to tell him the truth.

"Actually, yes, he does. He hasn't been the same since the

shooting. His behavior's been really unpredictable. I've tried to talk to him about it, but he brushes it off, says he's fine."

"He didn't look fine to me. He looked like he wasn't even there with us."

"I know."

"Well, what are we gonna do, Mama? We've got to help him." Morgan looked so upset. My heart broke for him, for all of us.

"What *you* need to do is stay out of trouble, Morgan."

"I know. I'm sorry, I was… I was just upset."

"I know you are. So am I. I want that guy caught just as badly as you do, but your dad is not well, Morgan, and you getting in trouble will only make things worse for him. Do you understand me?"

"Yes, ma'am. But I feel like I need to do something."

"Pray, Morgan. Pray for all of us, but especially for your father. Okay?"

"Yes, ma'am."

Nia's cries interrupted our conversation.

"Let me go get your sister," I said before kissing his cheek and leaving the kitchen.

I arrived in my bedroom to find Corey changing Nia's diaper. "You two okay?" I asked.

He nodded without looking up at me.

"Did she wake you up?"

"Yeah, but it's okay. I didn't sleep all that well, anyway."

I frowned. "Why?"

His hand began to tremble as he finished fastening Nia's diaper. He sat down on the edge of the bed and cradled her in his arms. He shrugged. "The hospital messed me up, I guess. There was always someone waking me up for this or for that. Never could get a good night's sleep. I just need to adjust to being back home."

"You sure that's all it is?"

His eye twitched. "What else could it be, Mo?"

"I don't—what did you just call me?"

"Huh?"

"You... you called me Mo."

"So?"

"In all the years I've known you, you have never called me Mo."

"Oh."

"Oh? Corey, what the hell is wrong with you?"

"Nothing!" he roared. The man had just gone from semi-catatonic to hulk mode in seconds. I watched as Lizzie, my poodle, jumped. She usually spent all of her time in Sahib's room. A second later, she scampered out of our bedroom door. I was sure she was headed back to her safe sanctuary.

I backed into the doorway. "O... okay. I'ma just go finish up with breakfast. You want me to take Nia?"

"Yeah. Let me know when the food is ready."

I nodded as I cautiously approached Corey and took Nia from him. As I left my bedroom and returned to the kitchen, my mind was troubled. I was worried about my husband. It was almost like he was a ticking time bomb with a very unreliable timer. I never knew when he was going to explode or what would set him off. He needed help. That much was clear. But he refused to even address the problem. What was I going to do?

As I finished preparing breakfast, my own hands trembled. I was afraid of the man who sat in my bedroom, a man whom I loved with every inch of my heart. I was afraid of my own husband.

***

I had just finished setting the table for Thanksgiving dinner when the doorbell rang.

"I'll get it!" Blair yelled.

Just as I was about inform everyone that dinner was ready, Blair walked into the dining room with a nervous look on his face. My heart began to beat in triple time. All kinds of dreadful scenarios flooded my mind as I tried to account for everyone's whereabouts. As far as I could remember, no one had left the house. Not Corey or Morgan—no one. Was it Wasif? Had something happened to him? Was that dream actually coming true?

My voice was shrill as I said, "What is it? What's going on? Is it your dad?"

He shook his head. "No, it's *your* dad. I... I invited him to dinner. He just arrived."

"What?!"

"He didn't have anywhere else to go, Mama. He was gonna have to spend the holiday alone."

"Is that the story you fell for? You believed him? Your heart is just too big, Blair. He's a liar. That's what he does—*lie*."

"Why would he lie about that?"

"Doesn't he still need a kidney?"

Blair shrugged. "He hasn't mentioned it. Look, Ma. He's a nice guy, and he's my grandfather. I just wouldn't have felt right if I hadn't invited him. No one should be alone on Thanksgiving."

I sighed. Blair really was too good a person. I wondered where he got his bleeding heart from. "Where is he?" I asked through another sigh.

"In the living room."

"Can you ask him to come here, please?"

"Mama—"

"*Now*, Blair."

His shoulders sagged as he turned and left the room. A few seconds later, my father appeared in the doorway. "Good evening, Mona-Lisa."

I cringed. The only person who ever addressed me by my full name was Corey and when he said it, it warmed my heart. Hearing my name roll off of my so-called father's tongue nauseated me.

"Look, I know you played on Blair's sympathies and wormed your way into having dinner here tonight. You can stay here and eat because I really don't feel like dealing with any drama right now, and

I don't wanna break Blair's heart since he actually believes you possess some human characteristics. This doesn't mean I give a damn about you and it sure doesn't mean I'm giving you a damn kidney. It's dinner. That's it."

He nodded with wide eyes. "I understand. I'm not asking for anything more. Thank you."

"Mm-hmm. Have a seat. I'm gonna call everyone else in here now."

As we all gathered around the table, anyone standing on the outside looking in would think we were a perfectly normal, happy extended family. No one would guess that Stella Sanders hated me or that her husband was her spineless follower or that my husband was unraveling more and more with each passing second. No one would believe that the man sitting across from me, who shared my DNA and some of my facial features, was the all-time heavyweight champ of deadbeat dads. No one could look into the faces of my four children and know the drama that was behind each and every one of their conceptions and births. And me—to look at me, one would never know how afraid I was of losing my husband at that moment.

As Corey said grace, I tightened my grip on his hand and said a silent prayer of my own. I prayed that whatever was haunting him, whatever was keeping him awake at night and causing his mood to shift, would leave him alone. I prayed for my lover and protector to come back and reclaim his body.

The dining room was enveloped in silence as we began to eat, and then the silence was replaced by the scraping of silverware against porcelain and the thud of heavy drink glasses settling against the table. I was just thinking how glad I was to be having such a peaceful meal when Stella spoke up. "So, Mr. Tolliver, you're Mona's father? I'm so glad to finally get to meet you. It was wonderful of you to come."

My father looked up from his plate and smiled. "Glad to be here amongst family. Good to meet you, too. Far as I can tell, your son is a good man."

I peered down at the table and kept my eyes glued to my plate as if its contents might run away if I didn't keep track of them.

"He sure is," Stella replied proudly. "What do you think about our new granddaughter? Just precious, isn't she?"

I looked up to see Mr. Tolliver smile and nod his head in agreement. "Yes, and she's beautiful just like her mother and her mother's mother."

My stomach dropped at the mention of my mother. There he sat, speaking of my mother like she was the great love of his life or something. What a load of crap! I took a bite of the fried turkey and then stabbed some green beans with my fork while fighting the desire to roll my eyes.

"Mona's mother?" Stella said, sounding intrigued. "I don't think we ever met her. Did we, Mona?"

I uttered "no" without bothering to look up from my plate.

"Well, she was a beauty. The prettiest girl at our school." He chuckled. "Being her boyfriend was like winning a prize. With Chrissy Dandridge on your arm, you were the man."

"Really? Well, if that's the case, Mona certainly took after her. She's always been so pretty," Stella said. "Mona, do you have any pictures of her? I'd love to see what she looked like." I looked up at her, my blood boiling from this man's little fake walk down memory lane. If *Chrissy* was so much, why'd he run at speeds to rival Usain Bolt's to get away from her when he found out she was pregnant with me? Lying sack of crap!

"No" was my curt reply. I hoped my voice conveyed the message that this was not a topic I cared to discuss.

"I have one," my father said.

My head snapped in his direction, and I watched as he pulled a picture out of his wallet. He slid it across the table to Stella who picked it up and smiled. "Oh, she was gorgeous! Look at that hair and her skin was flawless! Is this Mona with her?"

He nodded. "Yes, I think she was a little over three months old then."

I sat there stunned into silence. When I felt Corey's hand rest on my knee, I jumped.

"You okay, baby? You look upset," Corey whispered.

I didn't answer him. I watched Stella hand the picture back to my father, and I said, "I wanna see it."

He slid it to me and I stared down at it. My mother's smiling face stared back at me and yes, she was beautiful. Her hair was in huge ringlets that fell just below her shoulders. Green eyes that were replicas of mine and Morgan's and Nia's were filled with youthful hope. She held my chubby face close to hers. I felt tears begin to crowd my eyes as I turned the picture over and saw "Chrissy and Mona-Lisa" scribbled on the back in faded ink.

I looked up to see all eyes on me and then I scooted my chair across the floor with an unnerving screech and left the table without a word. I walked into the kitchen, leaned over the sink, and watched as bitter tears began to litter the stainless steel below.

Who the hell did he think he was? Where did he get off waltzing in here with a damn picture of me and my mother in his wallet? *Who the hell did he think he was?!*

I balled up my fist and slammed it against the counter. I had enough to deal with. I didn't need to see that picture of that woman looking like a real mother because as far as I could remember, she'd never *been* a real mother to me. And just how the hell did he get that picture? He was never in my life. *Never!*

I grabbed the clean dishes from the rack and raked them into the sink. And then I just stared at them. I picked up a knife and clutched it tightly.

"Baby, you all right?"

I turned to see Corey standing right behind me. I shook my head. "No."

"You want him leave?"

"No. I want him to come here."

His eyes shifted to the knife I still held. "Why?"

I looked down at my hand and almost involuntarily let the knife fall to the floor. "I need to ask him something."

Corey nodded, left the kitchen, and seconds later, returned with my father, who wore a look on his face that was somewhere in between fear and hope.

"Where did you get that picture?" I asked softly.

"From your mother. She sent it to me after I left."

I frowned. "Sent it to you? When?"

"After me and my family moved away. She knew how badly I wanted to stay. I loved her and I hated to leave but I didn't have a choice. I was just a kid. So she would send me pictures and letters. I... I still have them all."

I felt my face flush and my heart begin to race. "Why?"

He frowned, glanced at Corey. "Why, what?"

"Why are you standing here lying like you had some great romance with my mother?! Like you cared about her or me? Like you gave me a second damn thought! I *know* the truth. You knocked my mother up and then you ran like a coward and you never looked back! You didn't care then and you don't care now! So stop trying to pretend I am the product of love! I ain't nothing but the product of you not using a condom!"

He stepped forward and reached out his hand. "Mona, I'm sure your mother told you her side of things as she saw them. But did you ever stop to think that I had a side, too?"

I backed away from him. "First of all, *don't touch me.* Second, I don't give a damn about your side! I *know* your side! Your side let me grow up in abuse and misery and filth. Your side had sex with my mother right in front of me and my baby sister on the same sofa that I slept on every night. Your side let me get raped when I was a girl! Your side never called to wish me happy birthday or Merry Christmas or happy go-to-hell! Your side lurked your way back into my life only to ask for my kidney in return for absolutely nothing. Your side ain't worth a damn to me!" I yelled, banging my fist against my thigh with every word.

Corey stepped up next to me, slid his arm around my waist, tried to calm the uncontrollable trembling of my body.

"Mona, will you please let me explain? This is not about a kidney. I shouldn't have ever asked you to do that. This is about the fact that I don't know how much time I have left on this earth and I want to get to know you. I want to be a part of your life. I really mean that."

I shook my head as scalding tears began to inch their way from my eyes and trail down my cheeks against my will. "I. Hate. You. I *despise* you. Get out of my house." I didn't yell the words but, instead, let them slide off of my tongue evenly.

"Mona—"

"Get the hell out!!" I shrieked.

Before he could react, all three of my boys appeared in the doorway, and behind them, my in-laws—Stella with Nia on her hip.

"Let me walk you out, man," Corey said as he loosened his grip on me and moved towards my father. My father nodded.

My father shoved his hands into the pockets of his slacks. "I'm sorry. I never wanted to upset you. If you ever change your mind and decide to talk to me, Blair and Morgan have my number. I... I love you, Mona-Lisa."

That's when I lost it. I pounced on that man like a rabid dog. I tore into him, growling and biting and scratching. It took my husband, my two grown sons, *and* my father-in-law to pull me off of him. When the dust finally settled, I could feel his skin beneath my fingernails and taste his blood on my teeth. I could hear my two youngest children crying. I could hear the muffled voices of my sons saying something to me. I felt Corey's loving arms around me. I even heard Stella, of all people, praying for me. But my mind was gone, and left in its place was nothing but pure unadulterated rage. So much rage that I didn't think all the love in the world could extinguish it. I settled into Corey's arms and let my tears fall freely. And as the minutes passed, I could feel his love and comfort begin to brighten the dark spaces in my heart. Here he was with his own issues, but he was still with me, being the rock I needed him to be.

When we finally went to bed that night, he prayed with me and for me and I prayed for him. And when I drifted off to sleep, my mind was back, the rage was gone for that moment, and I was thankful.

14

"In My Heart"

I awakened the next morning to an empty house and a note taped to my bathroom mirror.

It read:

I thought you needed a little "me" time. So I'm seeing my mom and dad off and then me and the kids are heading over to the gym for a while to check up on things. Don't worry about Nia. I can handle her for a little while. Relax and get some rest. Be back soon. I love you.

-Corey

I smiled and then caught a glimpse of my reflection in the mirror. I stared at my face, remembering the picture. I remembered the smile that not only graced my mother's face but also shone through her eyes—*my* eyes. She looked so… happy. But I didn't understand how that could be. As far as I remembered, she was never happy—not *truly* happy. But that look in her eyes was one of pure happiness. And the way she held me, cuddled me so close to her. I almost believed that at that moment, she was glad to be my mother.

I shifted my gaze from the mirror and, after brushing my teeth and washing my face, headed to the kitchen to fix myself a solo breakfast. The house was almost too quiet and still. I actually missed the chaos and noise that usually surrounded me. I missed hearing Corey and the boys commentating on some ball game they were watching on TV. I missed Sahib tugging on my skirt or pulling on my leg, begging for some snack he couldn't reach on his own. I missed Nia's cries. I even missed her stinky diapers.

All of that, the busyness of my life, is what kept me sane. It kept my mind off of the other facets of my life—both past and present. With all of the noise and chaos, I found it impossible to focus on my past hurts. If there was just enough noise surrounding me, I couldn't think about the mother who had died without ever really apologizing for the things she did to me. I didn't have to think about her possessions, which had taken up residency in a barn on my sister's property. I didn't have to think about the rage I felt for my father. I didn't have to think about my husband's mental health or my own for that matter. I didn't have to worry about my children or their futures. I didn't have to feel bad about breaking Wasif's heart, either. But in the stillness and quietness, my mind was filled with those thoughts.

As if on cue, the sound of my cell phone buzzing and vibrating against the kitchen table sliced into the silence and pulled me out of my thoughts.

"Hello?" I answered.

"Good morning, baby. How you feeling?" Corey replied.

I settled against the back of my seat and tried not to cry. I loved this man so much. "Better. I'm sorry about last night."

"Don't worry about it. You're angry at him. Anyone could understand why. Look, I told him not to come back."

"Thank you. And thank you for giving me a break this morning. How's Nia?"

"Fine, fast asleep in her carrier. She's in my office with me."

"Office? I thought you were just gonna check things out. You're not working, are you? You're not supposed to be back at work.

And where's Sahib?"

"Look, baby, I'm fine. Hell, I actually feel halfway human sitting here doing something useful, and Sahib's with his father. Remember? Dr. Masood wanted to take him somewhere today. Blair dropped him off. "

"Oh. Where are Blair and Morgan, then?"

"Out on the floor, working out."

"Blair's working out?" I found that hard to believe.

Corey chuckled. "Actually, I think he's watching Morgan."

"Oh, well, I miss you guys. When will you be home?"

"In a few hours. Just relax, okay? Take it easy."

"All right. I love you."

"I love, you, too."

Almost as soon as I hung up my cell, the landline began to ring. I answered it and heard Stella's voice on the other end.

"Mona? This is Stella. We're on the road, and I just wanted to check on you. I've been worried. You were so upset last night. I just wanted to be sure I didn't do or say something to upset you."

I held the phone for a moment then replied with, "I'm fine. It wasn't you."

"Your father?"

"I guess that's what he is."

"Oh... uh..."

She didn't know what to say. She also didn't think I'd be able to see through her little act. Stella couldn't have cared less about me. She was being nosy. She just wanted to know what had transpired between me and my father that had led to me attacking him. Well, that was none of her business.

After a minute of silence, I said, "Well, y'all be safe."

"Um, all right. We're planning to come for another visit after the New Year."

"Okay."

I hung up before she could say anything else. I was calmer, but that didn't mean I wanted to play games with Stella Sanders.

I finished my breakfast, took a long bath, pulled on an old pair of jeans and a t-shirt and settled in my living room with a book. I'd drifted off to sleep when I heard the doorbell ring. I jumped up, a little disoriented. I stumbled to the front door and checked the peep hole. When I saw that it was Wasif, I was confused. He wasn't supposed to bring Sahib back until the next morning. Then something in my mind clicked. *Sahib.* Had something happened to him? I snatched the front door open.

"What is it?!" I looked down and saw Sahib standing there holding Wasifs hand. There was a bandage on his cheek. "What happened?" I asked.

"He slipped and fell down the stairs at Ann's house. He's okay. I gave him a few stitches. Fixed him right up but he wanted to come home. He wanted you."

I grabbed Sahib. "Ann's house? Stitches? *What?*"

"Um, I live with her now. Ann's really upset about this happening."

He lives with her? "She should be," I said.

Wasif sighed.

I squatted next to Sahib and kissed his cheek. "You okay, baby?"

Sahib nodded.

"Why don't you go on inside, sweetie? You can watch some TV if you want." I was trying to limit his TV watching but since he was injured, I figured it'd be okay.

He turned and waved goodbye to Wasif then trotted into the house.

I turned my attention back to Wasif. "Why weren't you watching him closer?"

"I just turned my back for a second, Mo. It happened really fast. You know I'd never let him get hurt on purpose. You *know* that."

It was my turn to sigh. "I don't know what I know about you anymore."

He frowned slightly. "What is that supposed to mean?"

"You are living with this woman? Marrying her? Why? I mean, I *know* you don't love her."

He shook his head. "What good is this discussion going to do? You left me. You moved on. That's what I'm trying to do. It's none of your business."

That last bit stung a little even if it was the truth. I felt my face heat up as I said, "Fine. Just don't let my baby get hurt again while he's in your care."

I turned and stepped back inside my house, slamming the door behind me without letting him reply. I walked into the den, sat on the sofa, and stared at my son. I wanted to cry but I had no idea why.

***

I rested my head against Corey's chest and closed my eyes. I'd enjoyed my day of rest for the most part, but my mind was still a little occupied. I sighed and silently prayed for a peaceful sleep.

Corey reached down and rubbed my arm. "You all right?"

I looked up at him and nodded. "Yeah. You?"

"I'm fine. You still upset about what happened to Sahib?"

I nodded. "He's just a baby and now he has stitches. Yeah, I'm *very* upset."

"He's okay though, right?"

"Yes, but if Wasif is gonna take him into a strange house, he needs to watch him closer."

"Strange house?"

"Yeah, evidently he's moved in with his fiancée," I said, trying to sound like I didn't care, but I really did.

"You don't say? Well, that's good. He's really moving on, huh?"

"Looks like it."

"Well, look. You know I don't like him, but I don't think he'd ever do anything to hurt Sahib."

"I know."

"What else is on your mind? Your father?"

"If you wanna call him that."

"Baby, maybe you oughta sit down and talk to him."

I lifted my head and looked him in the eye. "For what?"

"Maybe if you hear him out, it'll help you deal with your anger. Maybe you'll be able to forgive him. You need to do that, baby. You need to do that for *you*."

I was quiet. He was right and I knew it, but I wasn't ready to forgive my father. I wasn't ready to let go of the anger.

"I know you don't want to, Mona. But you need to."

"What about you?" I asked, shifting the conversation.

"What about me?"

I sensed a bit of an edge in his voice. I tried to measure my words carefully. "Do... do you need to talk to anyone about... anything?"

I felt his body tense. "Like what?"

"I was just thinking that what you went through was very traumatic. Maybe... maybe you should speak with someone about it."

"Someone like who? A shrink?"

"Well, yeah. I could call mine since you're already familiar with her from our counseling sessions."

"I'm not the one who needs counseling, Mona. I'm fine."

I sat up in the bed. "What is that supposed to mean? *You're* not the one?"

"I'm just saying, you need to deal with this stuff so we can move on."

"So we can move on? I'm holding us back? From what?"

He sighed. "Never mind. Let's just go to sleep."

"No. Answer me."

He sat up and switched on a lamp. "I'm just saying, Mona, your craziness is exhausting sometimes. Sometimes, I just wish things were normal."

"Normal? So I'm abnormal? Is that what you're saying, Corey?"

"No, you're just..."

I felt my whole body begin to tremble. "Crazy? Go ahead and say it again. *Crazy*."

"Okay. *Crazy*."

I balled up my fists. "And what do you think *you* are? You've been damn near schizophrenic since you were shot. I never know who's gonna wake up beside me in the morning—Dr. Jekyll or Mr. Hyde. Hell, at least I'm consistent!"

His eyes narrowed. "That you are. Especially when it comes to screwing your ex. I can always count on you to do that. You paid him for doing my surgery yet?"

I rolled my eyes. "Oh, here we go with that again. Paranoia on top of schizophrenia. And you're so damn mean now. You're like a walking mental institution."

"At least I'm not a whore."

"You would call your wife a whore? Really, Deacon Sanders?"

"Did I lie?"

I felt tears fill my eyes, willed them to stay where they were. "If that's how you feel, Corey, then why are you with me? If you are so sure that I cheated again, that I'm truly a whore, what are we doing? Why did you ever come home in the first place?"

"You know, my mama asked me the same question the other day, 'Why are you with her?'"

"What'd you say?"

"I told her I don't know."

I drew in a sharp breath. "Well, let me make this easy for you, Corey. Why don't I just take my babies and leave? That way we can end the damn mystery."

"Naw, you ain't taking my daughter nowhere."

"If you think I'ma leave her here with you, you have lost what's left of your mind."

"You can leave, but Nia stays. All you're gonna do is run straight to the good doctor. I don't want my daughter around him."

I stood from the bed, my worn nightshirt twisted on my body. I grasped the hem and began to twist it around my finger. "So you don't care if *I* leave? Is that what you're saying, Corey?" A single tear fell. "You don't love me anymore?"

He stared at me, and the cold expression in his eyes grew warmer. I saw a flicker of recognition, as if all of the words we'd exchanged had just, at that moment, registered in his mind. "Why would you ask me that? You know I love you."

I shook my head and backed away from the bed a little. "No, I *don't* know that. Not anymore. But I know you're tired of being with me. You just said as much."

He stood and walked around the bed. I backed away from him.

"You knew who I was, *what* I was, when you married me, and you said it didn't matter. You said that you loved me unconditionally—the bad and the good. I guess you were lying. I guess you didn't mean it. And I guess I should go," I said.

"Mona, I'm sorry. I didn't mean all that stuff. I'm just tired and frustrated. You know I love you. Haven't I proven that?"

A few minutes earlier, no one could've convinced me that Corey didn't love me. Now, I just didn't know. I crumbled. I stood there and dissolved into tears. That was all I could do. I cried because I knew what Corey had said about me was true. I probably was a whore. I had hurt him and the truth was, if it had come to it, I *would've* slept with Wasif to get him to do the surgery. So technically, his suspicions were correct. I could deal with him calling me a whore or thinking that I was cheating. What I couldn't deal with was the idea that he no longer loved me. I couldn't deal with that at all. So I cried.

Corey reached for me, pulled me into his arms. For a moment I relaxed against him. For a brief moment, I tried to forget the words he'd just said. I tried, but I couldn't. He was tired of me, he didn't know why he was with me, and maybe he didn't even love me.

"I'm sorry," he whispered as he held me close, stroked my back.

"You called me a whore. You said you'd never do that again," I whimpered.

"I don't know why I said that. I'm sorry, baby. I didn't mean it. I really didn't." He tightened his grip on me.

I knew he was lying. I knew he'd meant it. I *felt* it. I pushed against him a little. "Let me go."

"No, I can't."

I looked up at him. "Let me go. I need to leave. I need to get out of here."

"No, I'm not letting go unless you're coming to bed with me."

"I don't wanna be here, knowing how you really feel. Let me go."

He adjusted his arms around me, kissed the top of my head, then leaned over and pressed his lips to my ear. "I love you, *that's* how I really feel. I can't let you leave me. I'm sorry, baby." He released me and held my face in his hands. "I'm sorry."

I sighed. I was tired, it was late, and I just didn't have the strength to argue anymore. "Okay," I said. I followed him to bed, where he held me tightly until we both fell asleep.

***

I smiled as he planted soft kisses on the small of my back. Then he worked his way up to the back of my neck. "I love you," he whispered as he turned me over and covered my lips with his. We kissed for a long moment, both of us reveling in the bliss of our reconciliation, both of us eager for each other. I'd missed him, how we were always a perfect fit. He used to say I was made for him, *only* him. I used to believe that, too—that God made me just for him and him just for me. No matter how complicated things got, I always held on to that belief. I closed my eyes and listened to his declarations of love, felt his warm breath on my skin as he whispered them to me. Felt the electricity of his touch each time the pads of his fingertips caressed my skin. Felt his love in every kiss.

"Oh, Wasif," I murmured. "I... love... you..."

"I love you, too, babe," he replied as he—

I gasped as my eyes popped open. I was still in my bed, in my home, with Corey's arms wrapped around me. I glanced around the dark room, listening. But I had no idea what I was trying to hear. Wasif? An explanation of the dream? The echo of my own voice calling Wasif's name?

I gently pushed against Corey, he tightened his grip. "Unh-uh," he whispered.

"I need to check on Nia." We had moved her into her own room. I knew there was a baby monitor sitting right on the nightstand but I needed an excuse to get out of that bed.

"I'll check," he whispered.

I watched as he sat up on the side of the bed for a moment then stretched and stood up. He leaned over and kissed my forehead before leaving the room. I lay there in the darkness, trying to push the dream from my mind, trying to calm the violent thumping of my heart. I squeezed my legs together and tried to extinguish the heat that was rising inside of me, but as Corey walked back into our bedroom and reported that Nia was fast asleep, I realized there was only one way I was going to be able to extinguish the fire that was blazing inside of me.

So when Corey climbed back into the bed, I slid the nightshirt over my head and shimmied close to him. He smiled at me as I tugged at his pajama bottoms.

"This your way of saying you forgive me?" he asked.

I answered him by kissing his neck.

15

"Lately"

I sat in the parking lot outside of Sahib's school and sighed. Corey had spent the remainder of the weekend apologizing and being a very sweet husband to me, but none of that had erased the words he'd spoken to me. The fear and doubt was still there along with that one looming question that remained unanswered in my mind. *Does he still love me?*

I watched Sahib play on the playground and after the bell rang, I watched him file into the school with the other kids. Then I picked up my phone and dialed Cleo's number as I pulled off the lot.

"Well, hello!" she answered. "I tried to call you over the weekend. Everything okay?"

"I picked the wrong one," I replied.

"What?"

"The wrong man. I thought Corey was the one. Now I'm thinking I picked the wrong one."

I could hear her sigh. "Lord, what now?"

I told her about our fight and my dream. "That dream is a sign," I said.

"No, Mo, it was just a dream. And anyway, what are you planning to do, leave Corey for Wasif over one argument and a dream?"

"No, I think it's too late. Wasif's living with his fiancée now."

"Are you *serious*? You actually considered leaving him for Wasif?"

"Corey said some horrible things to me, Cleo. My ears are still burning."

"And he apologized, too. Look, I was trying to call you over the weekend because I realized something about Corey. I think he has PTSD."

I frowned. "From being in the service? That was years ago, why would it just now show up? Plus, he said he never really saw much action while he was enlisted."

"No, not from the Air Force. From the shooting."

I pulled my car to a stop in my driveway and thought for a moment. Maybe she was onto something. After all, she knew a lot about PTSD. She'd suffered from it herself. "Okay, suppose you're right. What in the world am I supposed to do? He won't even talk about what happened and me bringing up therapy is what triggered the last argument. I... I don't want to make him mad." I lowered my voice as if he could hear me from inside the house. "Cleo, he scares me when he's angry. He swells up and his eyes... he scares the hell out of me."

"Just try to talk to him again, *gently*. Maybe you could suggest couples therapy again. Maybe he'll be more receptive if he feels like it's not just about him."

I squeezed my eyes shut and rubbed my forehead. "Okay, I'll try. Thank you."

"No problem. Just be patient and don't give up on him. And no more of that nonsense about leaving him."

I sighed. "Okay, you're right. That was stupid. Love you. Talk to you later."

"Love you, too." I ended the call and walked into my house. No sooner than I'd closed the door behind me, I was greeted with, "Who the hell were you on the phone with!?"

I jumped, dropped my purse, and then squatted down to pick it up, my heart pounding in my chest. From that position, Corey towered over me like a giant. "M-my sister," I stammered.

"Let me see your phone," he demanded. I stood to my feet but before I could hand the phone to him, he snatched my purse from me and dumped its contents on the floor. He picked up my phone and began to check it, his breathing loud and erratic.

My eyes darted around the room. "Where's the baby?"

He didn't answer, engrossed in his current task. Satisfied that I hadn't been talking to Wasif, he handed me the phone. "What took you so long? Sahib's school isn't that far."

"I didn't realize I was gone that long."

"You erased the call, didn't you?"

"No."

I cautiously walked past him and made my way to my baby's room. He followed me, his breathing growing louder, more erratic. I reached her bedroom and peered over into the crib. She giggled and cooed at me as I lifted her from the crib. "Baby, please. I don't want to argue. I didn't delete anything."

He stared at me and for a moment, I thought that maybe he believed me.

I thought wrong.

He clenched his fists. A vein bulged in his neck. "I know you called him, Mona. Or did you go see him?"

"Corey—"

"Stop lying!" he yelled, and then brought his fist down on the baby's changing table. I jumped. Nia began to cry. I eyed the doorway.

"I'm not lying, Corey," I said softly, calmly.

He turned and began to punch the wall. "Stop lying!" he repeated. "Stop your damn lying, Mona-Lisa!" He punched the wall over and over again.

I backed into a corner, held my wailing baby against my body with an unsteady hand. "Corey, please stop!"

He didn't hear me. Or maybe he *couldn't* hear me. He kept punching that wall over and over again. The sound of the wood crushing under the force of his fists was deafening. The almost robotic way his arms moved was frightening. I cowered in the corner, tears of fear and confusion flooding my face as I tried to console my baby. But all at the same time, *I* needed consolation. Who would console me?

I watched as the crater in Nia's wall grew larger and larger, and I couldn't help but wonder if I was next. Would I be the next to feel the force of his fists? *I have to get out of here. I have to get to the door,* I thought. I slowly got to my feet and as I watched him, carefully began to ease toward the door. I was almost to the door when he turned around and his glower settled on my face. I froze. We stood there. The only sound in the room was Corey's breathing, Nia's frightened cries, and my own sniffling.

I held up a trembling hand. "Please... *please* don't hurt me. J-just let me go. Let me leave."

His expression softened almost instantly. He looked at me, then the baby. He held up his hands and inspected his torn, bloodied knuckles. Then he turned and looked at his handiwork—the hole in the wall. He turned back to me, tears in his eyes. "I'm sorry," he whispered. Then he slowly turned and left the room.

A few seconds later, I heard the front door close behind him.

***

I spent the better part of the morning trying to calm Nia's cries. And when she was finally calm, fed, and down for a nap, I tried to calm myself. But with every second that ticked away on the clock, I found myself staring at the front door or listening for Corey's vehicle in the driveway. The normal noises of my home were startling to me.

As I tried to go about my daily routine, I found myself shifting from tearful to fearful—back and forth. I was worried about Corey… and afraid of him. I wanted to call him, to be sure he was okay. But I was afraid to call him. Part of me wanted him to come home, another part of me was relieved he was gone. What was I going to do? Call him? Call the police? Report him missing? Call Cleo? The twins? The twins—thank God they were back at school. Thank God Sahib was at school, too.

I sighed. Just an hour until time to pick him up and I wasn't sure if I'd have my bearings in time to drive safely. My phone rang and I stared at it across the living room. What if it was Corey? What if it wasn't? I sat there so long that I missed the call but almost instantly, it began to ring again. Then a horrible thought hit me. What if he was hurt?

I stood from the couch and hurried to the phone to find that it was

Wasif calling, not Corey. And though Corey was gone, I was not sure if I should answer it. The phone stopped ringing. I released a breath. Then it started ringing again. *Wasif, again.*

My eyes darted toward the door as I answered the phone. "Hello?"

"Mo? You okay? You sound... scared."

My only answer was to sob into the phone.

"I'm on my way."

"No! No, please, *please* don't come here. Please don't. Please, *please,* Wasif!"

"Mo, calm down. What is going on?"

"Can you just pick Sahib up from school and keep him tonight?"

"Mo, what—"

"If you can't, can your fiancée get him? I... I can't." He'd have to know I was desperate to make that suggestion.

"Mo," he said, his voice softer, "Babe, what's wrong? What's going on?"

"Can you just please get our son for me?"

"Yeah," he almost whispered. "You need anything else?"

I shook my head and broke down again. "I d-don't know."

"Listen, I'll get Sahib and take him to my condo."

I wiped my tears. "Y... you still have the condo?"

"Yes. I'll be there if you need me."

I snuffled. "Okay... thank you."

"Mo, please call me if you need me. Okay?"

"Okay. W-why did you call me? Did you n-need something?"

"It... it doesn't matter. I'll talk to you later."

After we ended the call, I deleted it along with the one I missed. I wasn't taking any chances.

I sat in my house for most of the evening, nervously checking my phone and the door. I was so anxious that I nearly paced a hole in my bedroom carpet. Finally, I called Cleo. I needed to talk to someone, to tell someone what happened, or I was going to lose my mind.

She was barely able to say "hello" before I vomited out my words. I told her what happened, about Corey's outburst, his destructive rage. And then I cried into the phone—hysterical sobs. I could hear Cleo on the other end but I couldn't understand what she was saying. That is, until she screamed into the phone.

"Leave, Mo! Leave-right-now!" she shouted.

I stopped crying. "What?"

I could hear her having a muffled conversation with Scott. And then she returned to the phone. "Leave. Go to a hotel or come here, but you need to leave *now*."

"I don't think I can drive that far right now, to your house. But a hotel? Maybe I should stay. Like you said, he can't help it. He needs help."

"I know he needs help, but until he's willing to get it, you need to take your kids and leave. If he hurts you, it'll be too late to talk about him getting help."

"But—"

"Mo, *listen to me.* Yes, he needs help, and yes, he loves you, and if he was okay, if his mind was clear, he'd never hurt you. But he's not okay and you need to leave *right now.* Go to a hotel. Stay there. Me and Scott will come and get you in the morning."

"I... okay."

"*Hurry*, Mo."

I hurriedly packed a diaper bag and a duffel bag with clothes for me and Nia and some diapers and formula and then grabbed my purse and left. After I fastened Nia in the car seat, I tried to catch my breath and steady my hands, but they were still shaking as I backed out of the driveway and drove toward a hotel, *any* hotel. I checked in and got Nia all settled in the bed before I decided to call Cleo and tell her where I was. It was then that I realized I'd left my phone at home. My first thought was of Wasif. I knew he'd probably call to check on me. And I knew that if Corey intercepted that call, no matter how innocent Wasif's intentions might have been, there would be hell to pay. So I called him, told him where I was, and that I would call him later. Then I called Cleo, who promised to come and take me to her house in the morning. I told her not to hurry, that I felt safe for now. I took off my jeans, left on my t-shirt, and climbed into bed, exhausted from the anxiety and fear that had sieged me for nearly the entire day.

I'd just settled into a light sleep when I heard a soft knock at the door. I sat up in the bed and stared at the door. Who was it? Corey? I walked to the door, checked the peep hole, and was surprised to see Wasif on the other side.

I hesitated, still afraid of Corey and what he'd think if he found out Wasif and I were in the same hotel room at the same time.

He knocked again, whispered, "Mo, it's me, Wasif. Me and Sahib."

I checked the peep hole again and this time, I could see that he was holding our sleeping son. I opened the door, let him in, and quickly shut the door behind him. "Y... you shouldn't be here. You should go."

He laid Sahib down in the bed next to his sister. "I was worried about you. Why are you here? Where is your husband? What—who are you so afraid of? Sanders?"

I stared at him. I just couldn't say the words. Not to him. I couldn't tell *him* I was afraid of Corey.

Concern creased his forehead. He gently placed his hands on my arms. "Mo, you're trembling."

I hiccupped, let out a wail, and then came the tears.

Wasif wrapped his arms around me and pulled me close to him. He gently rubbed his hands up and down my back and whispered, "Oh, babe. Shh, it's okay." He gave me the consolation I'd been so desperate for. He held me and rocked me and soothed me. And when I finally stopped crying, he looked into my eyes and said, "I'm staying with you tonight. You shouldn't be alone."

I shook my head. "No, you shouldn't be here. Just *go*, Wasif. Please, go."

He held my face in his hands. "In all the years I've known you, I've never seen you this afraid of anything or anyone. I'm not leaving you." He turned, grabbed the key card from the night table, and headed for the door. "I'll be right back."

A few minutes later, he returned with a pillow and a couple of blankets. I sat on the side of the bed and watched him spread the blankets on the floor. "I won't touch you if you don't want me to. I just wanna be here for you. I wanna take care of you."

I nodded. "Okay." Lord knows I needed to be taken care of.

Wasif turned the light off and then settled onto his blankets and pillow. I lay in the bed next to my children and stared at the ceiling for a few minutes, not in the least bit sleepy. I turned and adjusted my covers and flipped back over.

"Can't sleep?" Wasif murmured.

"No."

There was silence as I continued to peer into the darkness. Then I felt the covers move. "Scoot over," Wasif whispered.

"What... what are you doing?"

"Helping you get to sleep."

There was only one sure-fire way he could do that, and there was no way *that* was happening. "Wasif—"

"Not that."

"Then what?"

"Move over and you'll see."

I hesitantly moved over and made room for him. He slid underneath the covers next to me and his fully-clothed body felt warm, comforting, familiar. He slid his arm across my waist and I stiffened for a moment, then I relaxed as I breathed in the scent of his cologne. He smelled heavenly and he felt good as he snuggled close to me.

I could feel his warm breath on the back of my neck as he whispered, "Yeah, just relax, babe."

He took his hand and began to softly comb his fingers through my hair over and over again. His hands felt *so good.* "You remember when I used to do this when you couldn't sleep?" he asked.

I closed my eyes. "That was a long time ago, Wasif."

"Not so long that I forgot. I don't think there's a thing I've forgotten about you. I don't think I *can* forget."

"Wasif?"

"Yeah, babe."

I yawned. "Why do you love me so much?"

"Because loving you is the one thing in my life that's always felt right."

My eyelids were too heavy for me to respond. He kept stroking my hair and whispering in my ear and before I knew it, I'd fallen asleep.

16

"Caught Up In The Rapture"

The night was rather restful despite the fact I was in bed with someone other than my husband. Nia only woke up twice to be fed and changed and Sahib slept like a log. As the sun began to peek through the curtains the next morning, I stirred a little and felt Wasif adjust his arm around my waist, tightening his hold.

I rested my hand on his arm and said, "Wasif, my sister's on her way to pick me up. I need to get ready."

"I broke off my engagement."

I rolled over to face him. "What? Why?"

"You have to ask? You know why. You know who I love." He kissed me softly and gazed deeply into my eyes.

"Wasif—"

He kissed me again, pulling me so close to him that I could almost hear his heartbeat. He kissed me and caressed me and I didn't stop him. I *couldn't* stop him.

He slid out of the bed and reached for me. I joined him on the floor where we kissed and caressed and undressed and groped, and we were right there, on the edge of reaching the point of no return, when a feeling of guilt hit me.

What am I doing? I wondered.

I closed my eyes as I pushed him away. "Wasif, I can't—"

"Come on, Mo. Don't do this. *Not now.* Just let me do this. I *need* to do this."

I shook my head. "No, I can't."

"Look, let's just do this and we can discuss how bad you feel about it later."

"Wasif, I really can't do this. I *won't* do this."

He rolled his eyes. "I know, I know. You *can't* and you *won't* because you're married to *him*. You love *him*. What I wanna know is why you're here with *me* and not *him*."

I sighed. "You can leave now."

"Really? You just get off on using me, don't you?"

I stood to my feet then sat on the side of the bed and redressed. "Oh, dear Lord. Not this. Not now, okay? I'm in the middle of a damn crisis and we have been over for years. Now, I'm glad you broke off your engagement because you had no business with that woman. She was just too... *nice*. But that does not change the fact that you blackmailed me into an affair, or that you married another woman *after* our sons were born. Corey ain't perfect, but he'd have to work overtime to catch up with the crap you've done."

He stood up and pulled on his pants. "Well, what *did* he do? What're you running from?"

"That is none of your business."

"It is if Sahib's safety is involved."

"Corey loves Sahib like he's his own child and you know it. He'd never hurt him."

"Do I know that for sure? After all, you called me begging for me to pick him up. Maybe I should just seek custody."

I glared at him. "Don't play with me, Wasif! Don't you even *think* about pulling some mess like that! Do you understand?!" I shouted, sounding like the mother bear that I was. I yelled so loudly that I woke up both Nia *and* Sahib and Wasif actually looked a little frightened.

Before either of us could utter another word, the room phone rang. Wasif grabbed the rest of his clothes and, with slumped shoulders, walked into the bathroom while I answered the phone.

"Hello?" I answered as I tried to tend to my babies.

"Mo, do you think you could hang at the hotel for another day?" Cleo asked.

"Uh, yeah, I guess. What's going on? Is something wrong?"

"Something's going on with Aaron. I'm so sorry, Mo. Just stay there for now. Don't go home."

"I understand. Take care of my nephew. Is he okay?"

"I just don't know. Listen, I've got to go. Love you. Be careful."

"Love you, too."

We hung up and I stared at the bathroom door. I wanted to go in there and cuss Wasif out for even thinking about suing for custody of Sahib. When he finally emerged from the bathroom, I was poised to do just that but his cell began to ring. Whoever was calling had just saved his life—or at least his ears.

I watched as Wasif answered his phone. He listened to the caller for a moment then looked over at me and said, "It's Morgan. He says he's been trying to reach you."

I frowned as he handed me the phone. I'd forgotten to tell the boys where I was and that I didn't have my cell with me.

"Hey, Morgan. I forgot to call you and Blair last night. I—"

"Ma, they called me and Blair last night trying to get in touch with you. Coach is in the hospital."

***

I was full of anxiety and guilt as I strode through the halls of the hospital with my baby on my hip. My heart felt like it was about to jump out of my chest. What was I walking into? Was my Corey back or would that stranger be there all full of anger, hurling accusations and insults at me. My stomach began to rumble as my mind shifted to Wasif and what we *almost* did, what I *would've* done had my sanity not returned to me. I stood on the other side of Corey's door, took a deep breath, and lightly knocked before opening it. I walked inside and tried to smile but all I really wanted to do was cry at the sight of Corey lying in another hospital bed, oxygen tubing wrapped around his face.

"Hey, Corey," I said softly.

He didn't speak back but just stared at me as I sat down next to his bed.

"Um, are you feeling okay?" I asked.

He shook his head and frowned as a single tear rolled down his face.

"No. I need you to leave, Mona. I don't want you here."

I blinked hard. *My* Corey was not the man who was lying in that bed. "But I want to be here. I'm your wife and I'm worried about you."

"I want you to leave and never come back. Just leave. Go on with your life. I'm no good to you now." His eyes shifted from my face to Nia. "I'm no good to either of you."

I stood and walked over to the bed. "I love you, Corey. Don't say that. I need you. *We* need you."

He sighed as another tear escaped his eye. "You need me? *Me?* I can't sleep because I keep seeing the gun—I keep feeling that bullets tear through my body. I keep seeing those kids falling around me—those kids that I couldn't help or protect.

"I can't walk for five minutes without getting out of breath. I tried to lift 20 pounds last night and I passed out—that's why I'm here. I feel so angry about everything and the anger won't go away. I keep dreaming about getting shot, dying. And... and I wet myself again last night because of a nightmare. I wet the damn bed again, Mona! I'm not a man anymore! I don't know what the hell I am, but I know I'm not a man. I can't be a husband or father if I'm not even a man!"

Then Corey did something I'd never seen him do before. He broke down in racking sobs. I laid Nia in his lap and he clutched her to him as I wrapped my arms around both of them. "You *are* a man. You're a wonderful, beautiful man. There's nothing wrong with you, Corey. We'll get through this. I'll help you."

He let me hold him and comfort him for a few moments before pushing me away. "No, I need you to leave. *Please leave, baby.*"

"Corey—"

"If you love me. If you love me at all, leave. Just leave, Mona-Lisa. *Leave.*"

"Corey, listen, I—"

"Damn-it, LEAVE!" His voice shook the walls around me and scared me out of my wits—scared Nia, too.

Without another word, I took my baby and left the room and pretty soon, I was in my car driving to my house in tears.

17

"Talk To Me"

It was hard convincing the twins not to come home to check on Corey, but I was finally able to convince them that the situation was not an emergency. He'd gone to the gym after his outburst at home and overexerted himself. The doctor had only admitted him as a precaution. I was relieved when they finally agreed to stay at school. I would've hated for them to encounter the rejection I encountered. They didn't need to see Corey like that.

Corey was discharged from the hospital the next day and when they called to inform me, I wasn't sure what to do. He had made it painfully clear that he didn't want me around. But what he wanted and what he *needed* were two different things. Even if he didn't want me around, I knew he needed me. So that morning, after I dropped Sahib off at school, I packed my baby up and headed for the hospital.

On the way there, I stopped by our church, hoping to have a word with the pastor and maybe solicit a little prayer. I could use all the help I could get if I was going to confront Corey again knowing he'd most likely reject me. I walked through the sanctuary to the pastor's office with my baby in my arms. His door was open and he just happened to be staring at the doorway when I appeared.

"Sister, come in!" he said. His smile was genuine, his voice warm.

I returned his smile and took a seat across from his desk.

"Brother Corey's been on my mind. How's he doing?" he asked.

I sighed. "That's why I'm here. Pastor, he's having a really hard time coping with what happened and the changes it caused with his body. He's been showing signs of PTSD, I think, and quite frankly, his behavior is scaring me. Plus, he's back in the hospital from over exerting himself physically. I just don't know what to do. I want to help him, but he's rejecting the help *and* me. I've made so many mistakes. You know I have. We've talked about them. When he's angry, which seems to be all the time these days, he loves to remind me of them. I know I'm not perfect, but I love him and I really want to help him."

Pastor Webb moved from his seat behind the desk to the one right next to mine. He reached for Nia. "May I hold her?"

I nodded and handed her to him.

He cradled her in his arms and kissed her forehead. He smiled at me. "Your family is a blessing."

"Yes, it is," I agreed.

"And Brother Corey loves his family. He loves *all* of you. He and I have had several discussions, and he always tells me how much he loves you and the children."

I nodded, fought back tears.

"And you love him," he said as he held Nia's hand in his.

"Yes, very much."

"Then fight for him. Fight for your family. Don't give up."

I released a ragged sigh as my tears began to seep from my eyes. "How do I do that? I'm on my way to pick him up from the hospital, but he's not gonna want me there. What am I supposed to do? I can't fight alone."

He leaned forward and covered my hand with his. "Sister, one thing I know about you is that you are not a weak-willed person. We've talked about your past. I know what you've survived. You're a *survivor*. Survivors *make* a way. Survivors don't take no for an answer. Survivors build skyscrapers with the bricks that people throw at them, and the devil has thrown plenty of bricks at you. Now it's time for you to show him what you and God can do with them.

"You know your husband. You *know* he loves you. He loves you and right now, he needs you more than ever. If he resists, you insist—*with love*. And with every move you make, remember that God is with you and that it is in His will for you to remain a family. Believe that and you won't fail. With him, you *can't* fail. The Word says in Matthew 19:26 that 'With man this is impossible, but with God all things are possible.'"

I nodded. "Thank you. Will you... will you pray with me... for us?"

He smiled again. "Of course."

***

I bypassed Corey's room and went to the nurses' station to sign his discharge papers and retrieve a wheelchair. Then I took a deep breath and headed for his room. Instead of knocking, I busted into the room—Nia's carrier in one hand while I pushed the wheelchair with the other. Corey, who was sitting on the side of the bed, snapped his head in my direction and opened his mouth to say something I was sure I didn't want to hear, so I interrupted him.

"You're all set to leave. They're sending you home on oxygen but you don't have to use it unless you need it. No new medicine." I parked the wheelchair in front of him and smiled. "Your ride is ready."

"Mona, what are you doing here?"

Here we go. "They're discharging you so I'm taking you home."

"I thought I made myself clear. Didn't I tell you to leave me alone?"

I set the baby carrier on the bed next to him. "Yeah, well, when have I ever listened to what people tell me to do? And I'm your wife; that hasn't changed. You're going home with me. Get in the wheelchair."

His eyes narrowed. "I don't know who you think you're talking to—"

"I'm talking to the man I love, the man who loves me. You do love me, right? And you love our family, right? Well, Blair and Morgan are worried sick. What do you want me to tell them when they call? What am I supposed to tell Sahib? That you refuse to come home?" Yep, I pulled the kid card.

He stared at me and then slid from the bed to the wheelchair with a grunt. He rode to the car and all the way home without another word.

***

Corey was quiet at home, didn't have much to say to me. He played a little with Sahib and Nia, but for the most part, he was very quiet—almost reserved. I was both relieved and a little anxious. Was this just the calm before another storm?

I called my sister shortly before bedtime to check on things on her end. She said everything was okay but wouldn't elaborate. I knew that Aaron had been troubled for a while now, since the incident with his father. But up until that point, he'd just been withdrawn and quiet—almost reclusive. The times I'd seen him, he was polite and mannerable, but he wasn't a conversationalist. I wondered what was going on with him now. I made a mental note to remember him in my prayers.

"So how are *you*?" she asked after giving me the vague report on Aaron.

"I'm good. Corey's home."

"Where are you?"

"I'm home, too. He... he was in the hospital. When they discharged him today, I brought him home."

"What?! Why would you do that?! You know it's not safe!"

"I think I might have overreacted. I don't think Corey will hurt me."

"You never think they'll hurt you until they *do* hurt you, Mo. And once they do, you never get over it." I heard a slight tremor in her voice as she spoke.

"Cleo, he's not like Frank. My situation is different from yours," I said softly.

"I'm well aware of that." This time there was an edge to her voice. I'd upset her.

"Cleo, I'm sorry. I didn't mean to upset you."

"You know what, Mo? You go right ahead and do whatever you want. Just don't call me bothering me when Corey gives you a black eye or chokes you unconscious. I have my own problems to deal with."

Click.

I held the phone and stared at it. *What just happened?* I wondered. Did she really think my husband was in the same league with her ex? Had what I said really upset her that much? Or was it whatever was going on with Aaron that had her on edge? And why wouldn't she tell me what was going on with him? Why the secrecy? I sighed. I guess I just had a way of making people mad.

My mind reverted to my earlier argument with Wasif—his semi-threat, Corey's seemingly perpetual anger at me, the conversation with Cleo. Then I allowed my mind to drift to my father. To the picture of my mother. To my mother, herself. I did wish I understood her… at least a little. I wished she had loved me… at least a little. I closed my eyes, cleared my mind, and walked back into my living room where Corey was quietly watching a ball game with both Sahib and Nia in his lap. He looked up and smiled at me, and I joined them on the sofa.

***

I woke up out of the blue that night. My sleep had been deep and restful—no dreams or nightmares had troubled me, but still, I found myself awake at 1:00 A.M.—or at least that's what my bedside clock read. I rolled over to find Corey's side of the bed empty and almost instantly smelled the familiar odor of urine. My eyes clouded and my heart ached for my husband. I stood and quickly began to strip the bed. I left our room and checked on the kids on the way to the laundry room before heading back to my bedroom. I could see a light framing the bathroom door and I could hear the shower running.

I knocked then opened the door and cautiously walked inside. "Corey?" I said.

No answer.

"Corey, are you okay?"

Still no answer.

I slid the shower door open to find my husband sitting on the floor of the shower in his pajamas… crying. I stood there for a moment, not sure what to do. I'd seen a lot of things in my life, good and bad. I'd felt a lot of joy and a lot of pain. But nothing in my life had ever come close to this. He looked so, so… *vulnerable.* He looked so small—almost childlike with his head buried in his knees. I guess that's why my mother's instinct kicked in. All I could think to do was to hold him, comfort him.

I stepped into the shower—the lukewarm water pattering against my night shirt, quickly soaking through the worn cotton. I slowly sunk down on the shower floor next to him and placed my hand on his arm. He jumped slightly, gazed up at me with a frightened expression that almost instantly transformed into a look of sorrow.

"Mona…" he groaned softly.

I pulled him into my arms and held him tightly as he wrapped his arms around me and clutched me like I was a newfound treasure—precious and rare. We held each other until the water that rained down on us turned cold. He cried tears of anguish. I cried tears of love. I whispered in his ear that I loved him, that I always would. I begged him to talk to me. But with each word I spoke, his heartbreaking sobs grew louder.

Through the sounds of his sobs and the water spraying from the shower, I thought I could hear Nia crying. I didn't want to leave Corey, but I had no choice.

"I'll be right back. I think I hear the baby," I told him, and then I left the shower and shed my wet clothes, replacing them with one of my robes. I stopped by the kitchen, grabbed a bottle, and returned to our bedroom with Nia.

Corey was out of the shower, wet and naked, standing next to the bed—staring at the wet spot.

"I'll clean it," I said as I sat in a rocking chair.

He didn't reply. He didn't move. He just stood there and stared.

I laid Nia across my lap and changed her diaper, and then I laid her on my chest and watched Corey. Nia quietly fell back asleep without a bottle. It was if she knew her father needed the quiet. As if she knew what would come next.

"I was sitting on the bench next to Frederick, watching the game, giving him some tips, having a good time. I love watching kids when they work hard and have a good time doing it," he said, his eyes still glued to the bed.

I was afraid that if I interrupted him, he'd stop talking. So I said nothing. I just sat there and hoped he'd go on.

"They were winning. Frederick's boys were winning. He had his little boy sitting next to him. His boy, Keelin, he's seven. He was so proud to be sitting there between me and his dad. It was a good game, you know? A good game..."

He turned and looked at me, then walked over to where I was sitting and sat down on the floor right in front of me. He rested his back against my legs. I rested my hand on his head.

"I... I remember leaning over and asking Keelin about playing basketball. I think I asked him if he wanted to play when he got older. I didn't hear his answer because a gunshot blocked my hearing," Corey continued in a soft, even voice. "I jumped up and tried to figure out where it was coming from. There were people screaming and running all over the place—players, other kids, parents. I... I couldn't see, I couldn't figure out who had the gun. I turned around and saw Frederick pushing his son towards the exit. Keelin looked *so scared*. Then Frederick looked at me and I knew we were thinking the same thing—we had to get the kids out of there.

"I turned around and that's when I saw him. He was so young, maybe fifteen or sixteen. And his eyes. They were searching. They were searching for... for someone to... to *kill*. I could see the bloodlust in his eyes. He looked *evil*. I think our eyes locked for a second and then he looked away. He'd spotted someone—someone to kill. He turned the gun and shot this boy, one of Frederick's players. I watched the boy fall. I saw blood spread across the chest of his dark blue jersey. I just... I just stood there and watched as that boy took his last breath. I... I couldn't move. I just stood there and stared at him.

"When I finally looked up again, the boy with the gun was staring at me. And then he lifted the gun to point it at another boy. Somehow, I managed to move. I pushed that boy down on the floor. That happened over and over again, the boy would point his gun at someone and I would push them out of the way. And then I turned to him and he was staring at me again. I could see the same determination in his eyes. And I could see anger. I knew... I knew that the anger was for me. He was... he was angry at me for helping those kids. And when he lifted the gun again, he pointed it right at me."

Corey got on his knees and turned around to face me. His eyes were full of tears; his brow was creased into a network of deep grooves. He placed his hands on my knees and continued to speak. "I stared at that gun in his young hand and the first thought that ran through my mind was of you and my children. I... I closed my eyes and I thought about how much I loved you—*all of you*. I wondered if you knew it, if you and the kids really knew how I felt about you, what you mean to me. I wondered if I was a good father to them and a good husband to you." A single tear rolled down his cheek.

"I wondered about the baby that was still inside of you. I wondered why I was being taken away from her. The bullets hit, one-two, real fast—almost at the same time, and it seemed like everything slowed down. When the bullets hit me, it felt like someone slammed a two-ton sledge hammer into my chest. They knocked the breath out of me and they knocked me off my feet. I heard Frederick call my name a few times as I struggled to breathe but I just couldn't catch my breath. *I just couldn't breathe.* It felt like someone, someone heavy, was standing on my chest. My chest felt so... so *full* and at the same time, it felt like there was an explosion going off inside of me, like my lungs and my heart were being blown to bits.

"I laid there and struggled to breathe and then I heard another gunshot and I... I didn't hear Frederick anymore. I tried to turn my head to look for him, but it was taking all of my energy just to try to breathe. Then I heard this horrible sound, a hissing, gurgling sound. And I realized it was me, it was the sound of me breathing. I heard someone close to me moan and I saw this girl out of the corner of my eye. She was crying, saying something I couldn't understand. Her face was so bloody. I remember thinking that she was going to die and I wondered if she'd accepted Christ. I wanted to lead her to him, but I couldn't speak.

"The last thing I remember before everything went black is

thinking, *please, God... please, God... please, Jesus. I'm not ready. I'm not ready...*"

He buried his face in my lap and wept. I rubbed my hand across his head as my own tears flowed, and I said, "Thank you for telling me, baby. Thank you so much."

18

"Whatever It Takes"

I felt dragged out and tired the next day, and Corey looked like he felt the same. We hadn't gotten much sleep and, as we sat at the dinner table across from each other with heavy eyelids, it was all either of us could do not to fall asleep. When we finally climbed into bed together, I closed my eyes and wrapped my arm around Corey as he led our nightly prayer.

"Heavenly Father, thank You so much for the many blessings You've given us. Thank You for the love that flows through our home. Thank You for protecting our family. Please bless us to have a restful night. Thank You and it is in Jesus' name we pray. Amen."

I closed my eyes and, even though I was sleep deprived, found it inexplicably hard to fall asleep. I raised my head and peered at Corey's face. His eyes were closed but I could see a small smile creep across his lips.

"What's on your mind, baby?" he asked.

"Can I ask you a question?"

He opened his eyes and fixed them on me. "What is it?"

"I was wondering if I could make a deal with you."

"Oh, Lord..."

"No, listen. I'm very thankful and proud of you for telling me about what happened."

His body stiffened a little. "Th... thank you for listening."

"Would you... would you be willing to see a counselor?" I asked timidly.

He moved his arm from around me and sat up in the bed with a sigh. "Mona—"

I sat up beside him. "No, listen. If you agree to see a counselor, I'll talk to my father. I'll... I'll listen to him and be nice to him."

He reached over and turned the lamp on. He stared at me for a moment. "Are you serious?"

I nodded. "Yes."

He sighed again. "Wow, I don't know what to say."

"Say yes. *Please,* say yes. I just want you to get better. I love you, Corey. I will do anything to make things better for you."

"I see. What if I agree to counseling with Pastor Webb?"

"Okay, how about this? You talk with him, if he thinks he can handle it, fine. If he thinks you need to talk to someone else, you'll agree to it."

He hesitated, and then said, "Okay."

I released a relieved breath. "Thank goodness. If that didn't work, I was gonna start offering sexual favors as a bargaining chip."

He smiled then leaned over and kissed me. "Can we renegotiate, add the sexual favors as a bonus?"

I giggled. "How about I just throw that in, anyway, for good measure?"

He lay down and pulled me to him. "I'd like my good measure

now, please."

He kissed me deeply. I closed my eyes and thanked God for the little bit of light that was peeking through the end of the tunnel.

***

I'd been trying to call my sister for two weeks. I wanted to tell her about Corey's counseling sessions and how well he was doing. I wanted to tell her I'd called and gotten my father's phone number from Blair. But most of all, I wanted to check on Aaron.

I kept getting her voicemail when I called her cell phone. When I called her landline, either Scott or one of her younger kids would answer and inform me that Cleo was either busy or gone. When I asked Scott about Aaron, he told me he was better. *Better than what?* I wondered. My heart was aching. I missed my sister. The rift that was forming between us reminded me of the years in the past when I was left wondering if she was alive or dead. There had been a huge hole in my heart during that time. It was a hole that neither my boys nor Wasif nor Corey had been able to fill. It was only when I rushed outside my house and stood face-to-face with my sister a few years ago that the hole began to close. But now I could feel the healed edges began to pull apart. I could feel that familiar ache return to my soul and I just didn't know what to do about it.

I sat in my kitchen, the phone in one hand, the phone number I'd haphazardly scrawled on a piece of paper in the other. I'd spoken to my twins, Sahib was at school, and Nia and Corey were napping. There was nothing left to do and after all, I *had* promised Corey. So, with much trepidation, I dialed the number and held the phone to my ear. *One ring, two rings,* and just as I exhaled in anticipation of the voicemail picking up, I heard, "Hello?"

I held the phone and my tongue. This was a mistake. No matter what I'd promised Corey, this was a mistake. *I should hang up. I should hang up right now.* My thoughts came in rapid-fire succession. But my hand didn't move.

"Hello," my father repeated.

"Hello?" I finally said.

"Hello?" he repeated again.

We were beginning to sound like a couple of hearing impaired elderly people, parroting that one word over and over again.

"Uh, this is Mona. Did Blair tell you I was going to call?"

"Y... yes. Yes, he did."

"Um, how are you?"

"I'm fine. How are you?"

"Fine."

Silence.

I didn't know what to say next and neither did he, evidently. After a few more minutes, I decided to end our mutual torture. "Well," I said, "I guess I'll call you another day, see how you're doing then."

"Uh... uh, the boys say they're going home this weekend—to visit."

"Yes, they are."

"Do you, do you think I could come with them? I'll get a room at a hotel, but maybe I could visit with you this weekend. With all of you."

I closed my eyes, tried to steady my breathing. I did not like this man—not even a little bit. But I loved Corey and I'd made a deal with him. He'd held up his end. Now it was time for me to pull on my big girl panties and hold up my end. I massaged my forehead as I said, "Sure. That'd be fine."

Then I ended the call and hoped I'd spoken the truth. I hoped everything would, indeed, be fine.

19

"More Than You Know"

I was darn near hyperventilating by the time I made it to the door to answer the doorbell. I knew it was my boys. Despite having keys to the house, they always rang the doorbell when they came home for a visit. It was a little game we played. They'd ring the doorbell and I'd interrogate them through the door, pretending that I didn't know who they were. Usually, Sahib would be next to me, grinning from ear to ear, waiting to see the two big brothers he idolized. When I finally opened the door, my boys would converge on me and all of us—me, the twins, Sahib—would embrace in a group hug. The first time they came home for a visit, I cried for an hour. I'd missed them so much. For all the years I was Wasif's mistress, I spent most of my time raising or thinking about my boys. They were my life for so long. They were my everything.

But this time, as I stood at the front door, my anticipation was clouded by apprehension. I couldn't breathe or think and I honestly wanted to run and hide underneath my bed. I didn't want to face him—*my father*.

Sahib stood next to me and when I looked down at him, he looked confused, probably wondering why I was standing there staring at the door in silence. That's when I snapped out of it. I cleared my throat and croaked out, "Who is it?"

I looked down at Sahib and watched a smile take over his small face. That smile lightened the load on my heavy heart. The twins and I bantered back and forth for a couple of minutes and then I opened the door and feigned my surprise. As we all hugged, I closed my eyes and pretended not to know that my father was standing behind my sons, staring at me. Morgan grabbed Sahib and all three boys rushed to the living room to see Corey and Nia, leaving me alone with *him*.

I smiled weakly. I could feel my heart beat in my throat. "Um, come in."

His expression went from tense to relieved. I guess he didn't know what to expect from me. Judging from how I'd pounced on him before, I couldn't really blame him. We walked into the living room and, thankfully, my father, husband, and sons became engrossed in a college basketball game on television. After a few minutes, I was able to slip out of the room undetected.

I walked into the kitchen and breathed easily for what felt like the first time in hours. I sat at the kitchen table, closed my eyes, and clutched my forehead.

"I want to show you something. May I sit?"

I looked up to see my father standing over me. I nodded. He sat across from me, pulled an envelope from his pocket and slid it across the table to me. I stared at it for a moment before picking it up.

It was pink, faded pink. I opened the envelope and slid the photograph out. It was a photo of my mother. She was very pregnant and appeared to be very happy. She was smiling widely, her hand resting on her stomach. I turned the picture over and read the words penned in my mother's big, loopy cursive handwriting: *Chrissy, 7 months pregnant.*

I stared at the picture—at my lovely, hateful, abusive mother. I stared at her smiling face and her huge stomach.

"I don't understand," I whispered.

"What don't you understand?" he asked.

"She looks so happy. I don't ever remember her being happy."

He frowned a little. "She was... for a while."

I continued to stare at the picture. "I wish I'd known that side of her."

"I'm sorry you didn't."

"Do you know what happened to her? What made her change into such a horrible person?"

He cleared his throat, ran his hand over his thick, graying hair. "I know she had a rough childhood. She suffered a lot of abuse. I guess that stuff just comes out eventually."

"But she wasn't like that with you?" I asked. "She wasn't mean and angry?"

"No, she loved me. We... we loved each other. *Very much.*"

I felt tension building in my head. I shook my head. "She said you took off as soon as you found out she was pregnant. She never talked about love."

"She was angry with me. I... I hurt her. I didn't mean to, but I did. I... I left her."

"You moved away?"

"Yes. My parents moved me that summer before you were born. I had full intentions of being there for her, for both of you. It just didn't work out that way. She wrote for a while, sent pictures. Then she just stopped. Next thing I knew, my letters were being returned. She'd moved."

I closed my eyes. I had a lot of questions for him. I wanted the answers, but I needed a break. I needed some air. "Can we... can we talk later? I don't feel too well."

"Oh, sure. I'll just... I'll just go now."

"Okay."

I didn't bother to walk him out. Instead, I walked out the back door and sat on the steps. I closed my eyes and tried to clear all of the unanswered questions from my mind.

"Mind if I join you?" It was Corey.

I shook my head. "No."

He sat down beside me and grasped my hand. "You okay?"

"Not really. I talked to him and now I feel like crying."

"Then cry, baby. There's nothing wrong with crying."

I leaned against my husband. And I did just that. I cried.

***

I sat and stared at my cell phone as it rang, not really paying attention to it. Corey, the twins, and my father were all gone to a local sports bar to watch some basketball game together. Nia was napping. My sister still wouldn't talk to me, and my mind was still trying to absorb the possibility that my mother had, at one time, actually been a feeling human being. It was hard for me to understand it.

Actually, I didn't want to believe it. Believing that my mother was a heartless witch had enabled me to keep my sanity through the rough times—the times when she disregarded my basic, human needs to fulfill her carnal needs. Seeing her as less than human kept my rage at bay—kept me from believing that I deserved to be treated that way. She *had* to be inherently evil. What other explanation was there?

I closed my eyes and rested my head on the back of the sofa. I let the quiet of my home fill my ears, hoping it would quiet the constant noise in my brain. I would talk to my father again when he and the rest of my family returned home. I would learn all I could about my mother's past, her abuse. Maybe then I would understand.

My phone began to ring again. This time I checked it and saw Wasif's name flash across the screen. Sahib was with him. I answered hoping nothing was wrong.

"Hello?"

"Are you avoiding me?" he said.

I frowned. "What? What are you talking about?"

"Your husband dropped Sahib off. The same husband you were afraid of a few weeks ago."

"So?"

"So... are you avoiding me?"

"No."

"Then why didn't you bring him?"

"Because Corey and the boys were headed in your direction anyway. I thought it'd make more sense for them to drop him off and I thought maybe you'd like to see the twins."

"No, I think you're avoiding me."

I sighed and thought to myself that I didn't have the time or the mental capacity to deal with Wasif and his paranoia. "I can't, Wasif. I can't do this with you right now."

"I poured my damn heart out to you about Ann and you don't have time?"

"Have you lost your mind, Wasif? Have you gone completely crazy? Are you seriously doing this right now?"

"I was there when you needed me. I dropped everything and *I was there*. The least you could do is return the favor."

I sighed. "Wasif..."

"I don't know what I'm doing. I still miss you. All this time and I still miss you. I thought being with someone else, *anyone else,* would change things. But it didn't. I didn't love Ann for the same reason I couldn't love my wife—neither of them were you." His voice broke ever so slightly as he spoke.

"Wasif—"

"I know we're over. I know you love him, but that night—you were so scared and when we were together in that bed, it felt like, it felt *real* again. Like I could have you again. When I saw him tonight, grinning and happy, it hurt, Mo. It *still* hurts."

"Wasif, I don't know what you want me to do. I don't know what I can do to make things better for you. I'm... I'm sorry. I never meant to hurt you again."

"I guess I know that. It hurts just the same, though. I just… I wish you still loved me."

"I do, Wasif, and I always will. You *know* that. But this is the way things are, the way they have to be. I'm Corey's wife. I belong with him."

"Yeah, I know," he said softly.

"How is Sahib?" I asked, trying to redirect the conversation because I seriously could not deal with the drama at that point.

"He's fine. Playing a video game. Look, I'll let you go."

Thank God. "Okay."

"You know how I feel so I won't say the words."

"Yeah, I know, Wasif."

I hung up and clutched the phone in one hand, my head in the other. I closed my eyes. I didn't need this. I didn't need to hear Wasif sounding so pitiful. Not now. Not when my own mental state was so fragile. I took a deep breath and released it and as I opened my eyes, I saw Corey standing over me with fire in his eyes.

20

"Only For A While"

It wouldn't take a genius to know that Corey had heard at least part of the conversation—the part where I said Wasif's name at the very least. I opened my mouth to offer him a truthful explanation. I wanted to tell him that Wasif had called me—not the other way around. I wanted to say that I'd declined Wasif's advances. I wanted to tell him that he had nothing to worry about, that I was his and his only. But the words wouldn't come. The only thing I could do was to stare into his eyes and plead with my own.

I watched the vein in his temple bulge and pulsate. I watched as his fists clenched then relaxed then clenched again. I watched as his breathing became more and more ragged.

"Corey," I was finally able to say. "Do you remember what the pastor told you about controlling your anger? Breathe, baby, breathe."

His brow furrowed. A single tear escaped his left eye. He remembered and he was trying to control it. "Why were you talking to him behind my back?" he asked in a shaky voice.

"I wasn't. He called about Sahib. That's all." Now was not the time for the truth. "Where's everyone else?"

Another tear rolled down his cheek. I could no longer see the vein in his temple. He believed me.

"Corey, where are the twins and my father?"

He turned and walked over to his favorite chair and sunk into it. He held his head in his hands. "The boys took him to his hotel so he could change clothes. He spilled beer on his shirt."

I frowned a little. "Should he be drinking beer with his kidney problem?"

Corey shrugged and I asked myself why I even cared.

"I'm sorry, baby. I just... hearing you say his name, it just set something off inside of me. And the way he looked at me when we dropped Sahib off at his place—like he thought I'd fallen off the face of the earth. I just thought something was going on. I'm really sorry. Thank you for helping me to calm down," Corey said.

I walked over to him and sat on the arm of the chair. "It's okay. You need the oxygen?"

He shook his head as he looked up at me. "I just need you. You're my oxygen. I love you, baby."

"I love you, too." I wrapped my arms around him and squeezed, thankful that that little episode was over.

***

"Chrissy was born and raised for years down in England, Arkansas before she moved to Little Rock, where I met her. Things were really different back then. Most white people didn't accept the fact that her white mother had kids by a black man. She suffered a lot of abuse from her mother's side of the family. She told me she hated them but she thought they hated her and her brother more," my father said then took a sip of his coffee.

I looked up from the table where I had fixed my eyes on yet another picture of my mother. "Brother? She... she has or had a brother?"

He frowned as he sat his mug down. "Yes. Kenny Ray. You never met him?"

"I never knew she had a brother at all."

His eyes widened. "I wonder why she didn't tell you. She and Kenny were very close. She kind of took care of him when they were young."

Like I took care of Cleo? I shook my head, gave him a wry laugh. "Wow, that woman was something else. I have an uncle that I've never heard of. I wonder why my grandmother never mentioned him." I paused. "I wonder if he's still alive."

He shrugged. "Last I heard, he was. But that was before you were born. She didn't mention him the next time I saw her. The time you first met me." He dropped his eyes.

"Okay, since you brought it up. What was wrong with you that day?"

He sighed. "To be perfectly blunt with you, I was probably high as a kite."

"I figured you had to be."

"I'm... I'm sorry. I've done some pretty stupid stuff in my life. I was in a real bad place back then. I'd finished college in California and I thought sure I'd get into the NBA. When I didn't, I took it real hard. I came back home—to Little Rock, and ran into a mutual friend of me and your mom's. He told me where she was living and I just kind showed up that day."

"And you had sex with her in front of my baby sister," I said through a throat that was partially constricted by bitterness.

"I didn't go there for that. I wanted to talk to her and to see you. But your mama was a gorgeous woman and I guess I just was too high to think clearly." He shook his head. "Look, I don't want to make any excuses. There's no good reason for exposing myself to you and your sister. All I can do is apologize now. I'm sincerely sorry."

"Why didn't you come sooner? I was 6 years old by then."

"I was selfish, stupid, young, and dumb. After your mother lost touch with me, I just shut down and started thinking only of myself. I kept my mind on basketball and my future."

I shook my head. "Didn't you ever wonder about me or how I was being treated? I couldn't imagine going any more than a day without knowing how my kids are doing."

He looked me in the eye then shifted his gaze to the table. "I thought your mother would take care of you. I thought that's what all mothers did. It never occurred to me that you'd be mistreated."

I leaned back in my chair and bit my bottom lip to keep from screaming. "So that would be a no, right? You didn't think about me."

"No, I'm sorry to say that I didn't. At least not in the way you mean. I wondered how you looked, if you looked more like me or your mother. But that was about it," he said softly.

"And all these years, up until two years ago when you came begging for my kidney. All the years after the first time you saw me, did you think of me?"

Silence.

I felt it again—the rage, the anger, the hatred. With his silence, he'd answered my question loud and clear, and I hated him because of his answer. "If you didn't need a kidney, would you have ever tried to contact me?"

"I... Yes. I would have eventually."

There it was. A lie. The first one of the evening. Everything else he'd said I believed to be true. But this was a lie. Had his poor health not demanded it, he never would have sought me out. And that lie did it. It unraveled the tightly-knitted composure that had kept me from screaming at him or kicking him or punching him. I stood from the kitchen table, my hands trembling and my head throbbing. "Since you wanna start lying, you can leave now," I said evenly.

He looked up at me. "I'm sorry, Mona-Lisa. I wish I could say that I've been looking for you all the time. I wish I was a better person before, but I wasn't. I'm a better person now and yes, it's because I'm sick. Maybe God had to bring me to this in order for me to see how wrong I've been, to see the mistakes I made. But I'm here now and I sincerely want to get to know you. For however much time I have left, I want to be a father to you."

"Get. Out."

"Will you just listen for a moment—"

"Get the hell out!!!" My voice sounded foreign in my own ears. For a moment, I almost thought someone else had shrieked the words. But when my twins and my husband ran into the kitchen and stared at me, I knew it was me.

"Baby..." Corey said softly.

I felt a single, warm tear course down my cheek. "I didn't ask to be brought into this world. I wasn't a bad child. I tried to be a good girl. I really did. Why couldn't you or my mother just love me? Why was that so hard?"

"I *do* love you. I'm sorry, Mona-Lisa. If I could go back in time and change things, I would. *I'm sorry.*"

"You didn't care. You never cared and I just don't understand. I don't understand why you couldn't have been there. I don't understand why she had to be so hateful." I dropped to my knees in a mass of tears. "I need to understand. I thought you could help me, but you can't." Corey rushed to my side and pulled me into his arms as I sobbed loudly. "What was so wrong with me that you didn't even care if I was living or dead until your life depended on it? *I need to know.*"

"It wasn't you. It was *me*. I was selfish and stupid. I know there's nothing I can say to take your pain away. I know that but I wish I could, baby girl. I really wish I could." There was a tremble in his voice. I looked up to see tears wetting his face. He kneeled beside me. "*I'm sorry.* You didn't do nothing to deserve my neglect. That was all me." He slapped his hand against his chest. "*Me*, not *you*. There's nothing wrong with you. You're beautiful. I could see that in those pictures your mama sent me. I saw it that day when you were six. I just never thought your mother would mistreat you and I was so messed up back then. I didn't need to be in your life."

All I could do was cry. Corey continued to hold me and then I felt another set of arms around me, heard someone else's sobs. I didn't have to open my eyes to know that my father was also holding me and crying with me.

"I'm sorry, but if you'll let me, I'll spend the rest of my time on this earth making it up to you. I'm sorry. I'm sorry. Please forgive me. Please forgive me…"

I let him hold me. I let him cry with me. And when I finally pulled myself together and looked at him, I saw him for what he really was—a broken man. A broken man with more regret left in his life than years. And as much as my heart ached for myself, it also ached for him. I wasn't perfect by a long shot, but I had done my best to love and nurture my kids. Of all the things I had to repent for, neglecting them was not one of them. That was more than he could say.

After the twins took him back to his hotel that night and I'd settled down in my bed, I prayed for God to heal the wounds inside of me, to seal up the hurts of my childhood. And believe it or not, I prayed for my father, too.

21

"Angel"

"I'm sorry. She's not home right now, Aunt Mo."

I sighed at hearing those words from my nephew—my sister's son, Shane. "Is your father home?" I asked.

"Yes, ma'am. Just a second."

The next voice I heard was my brother-in-law's baritone twang of a voice. "Hello?"

"Scott, it's Mo. Is... is everything okay? How's Aaron?"

"He's... better."

"Look, I know my sister is mad at me, but I really need to talk to her. I'm worried about her and Aaron." I felt my eyes swell with tears. I was lost without her.

"I'm sorry, Mo. She just doesn't want to talk to anyone."

"When will she be back home?"

"I'm expecting her in a couple of hours."

"Okay, thanks." A couple of hours was just long enough.

***

I looked over at Corey and sighed. "I'm sorry for asking you to do this right now. I know you don't feel your best but—"

Corey shook his head and rested his hand on top of mine. "Don't worry about it. I'll be fine."

I nodded, took a deep breath, and said, "Well, come on then. Let's do this."

As I reached to open my door, Corey gently grasped my arm. "Hey, everything's gonna be okay, baby. I love you."

I smiled. "I love you more."

A few minutes later, we were standing before the front door of a stark white, two-story farm house. I knocked and waited. Then I knocked again. A few seconds later, the door opened to reveal my brother-in-law wearing a forlorn expression on his face.

He sighed and shook his head. "Mo—"

"Don't," I said. "Don't say she's not here. Her car is in the driveway. I know she's here, Scott. I'd like to see her, please."

He dropped his head and fixed his eyes on the floor of his front porch.

"*Please*," I repeated.

He looked up at me and nodded. "Stay here. I'll go get her."

I breathed a sigh of relief. "Thank you."

I looked over at Corey who gave me a little smile and a nod. I turned back toward the door in time to see my little sister open it. She looked so tired. Her hair was pulled into a loose ponytail. Her clothes hung from what looked to be a thinner frame. There were bags underneath her eyes. As she stood there and stared at me, I felt my heart begin to break for her. I wanted to reach for her, to pull her into my arms and rock her like I did when we were girls. But I was afraid to.

"Mo, I just can't do this right now. I just do not have the time or the energy for this," she said. Her voice wavered as she spoke. I could see tears as they shone in her eyes.

"We need to talk."

She shook her head. "Not today. Not right now. I can't."

"Can I please come in?"

"*Please*, Mo. Just... just go home. I'll call you when I can."

"I'm not leaving until you let me in. We need to talk."

"Mo—"

"Look, it's cold as hell out here and I've got an old poodle, a recovering gunshot victim, a baby, and a five-year-old with me. We drove all the way here because you refuse to talk to me over the phone. Can you *please* let us in?"

She looked past me and seemed to notice Corey, Sahib, and Nia for the first time. She backed out of the doorway. "Come in," she said with a deep sigh.

A few minutes later, I was sitting next to my sister in her spacious living room. Family photos with smiling faces surrounded us. We were alone, just the two of us. Our husbands and children had dispersed to other parts of the house, giving us some much needed privacy.

"How are things with Corey?" she asked softly.

"Better. You were wrong about him. He hasn't laid a finger on me. He would never do that," I answered.

Her eyes met mine. "How can you be so sure?"

"The same way you're sure Scott would never hit you. Even if he had PTSD, you *know* he'd never hurt you, don't you?"

"No, Mo, I don't. I know what it is to love someone and have them hurt you. Do I think the Scott I know and love right now today would hurt me? No. But I can't say what he would do if he was going through what Corey is going through."

I sighed. "I just don't agree with you, sis. I just don't."

"I wouldn't think that you would. You've never experienced what I experienced. You've never been slapped or punched or choked or stomped by the one person you believed loved you. You have no idea how that feels. You weren't there. Of course you disagree."

I dropped my gaze. "I... I wish I'd been there for you. I wish for that more than anything in the world. I would've protected you just like I always did. I hate what that man did to you. But Corey is not him. I know he wouldn't hurt me. I need you to trust my judgment on this."

"How can you know he won't hurt you? How can you *know* that?"

"Because he said he wouldn't, because his heart is pure, and because he loves me. Besides, if he really wanted to kick my butt, I have given him several reasons to throughout the years. I figure if he hasn't already done it by now, I'm safe."

She gave me a tired smile. "I don't wanna fight you anymore. If you truly believe you're safe with him, I trust your judgment. No one knows him better than you."

I smiled. "Yes, and I didn't get to tell you how well his counseling is going. He's really doing good. Wasif still sets him off, but he's learning to control his anger."

"That's really good, Mo. I'm happy for you two."

I reached over and rested my hand on top of hers. "Tell me what's been going on with Aaron."

She sighed again.

"Please, Cleo. Please let me help you carry whatever this burden is that you're carrying. I can tell it's too heavy for you to carry alone."

She looked up at me as her tears began to flow. "Did I tell you that I've been looking for my father?"

I frowned a little, confused as to what this had to do with Aaron. "No, you didn't."

"Believe it or not, I envied you. I envied the fact your father found you, no matter *why* he found you. At least he put forth the effort. That's more than I can say for my father." She leaned forward and clasped her hand over her forehead. "So I've been surfing the web looking for Donald Williams. It's a common name—*too* common. Scott even got his cousin at the Sherriff's Department to help. But since I don't even have a copy of my own birth certificate or know this man's birthday or middle name, it's like looking for a needle in a haystack. But that didn't stop me.

"That's what I was doing when it happened. I was on the Internet trying to find a Donald Williams, *any* Donald Williams."

Her tears began to fall more rapidly. I wrapped my arm around her shoulder. She blew out a breath and continued. "I was sitting at my computer when I heard the gunshot. I sat there and it felt like the blood drained from my body. It... it's not like a gunshot is rare around here. Everyone in my house knows how to shoot a gun, including Serenity. But in my being, I just knew that *this* gunshot was different. I knew something was very wrong. Then I heard Serenity's voice. She was screaming bloody murder. I ran from my office out the back door. I ran towards her voice, and there he was, my baby, lying on the ground in the forest behind my house with blood of all over the side of his head."

I gasped. "Oh, no, Cleo. *No, no, no...*"

"He was alive," she continued. "Shane had followed him out into the woods, and when he saw him put the gun to his head, he jumped out and startled him. Aaron pulled the trigger but the bullet just grazed his head. You see, Shane was paying more attention to Aaron than I was.

"When Aaron decided to stay here and learn how to run the farm instead of going off to college, I was so relieved because he'd be home and I could watch him. Now I'm thinking that wasn't a good idea. Maybe being here was a constant reminder to him of what happened." She wiped her face. "What kind of mother am I that I didn't see how depressed he really was?"

I shook my head and squeezed her hand. "Don't do that to yourself. This is *not* your fault. You tried and tried to talk to him, offered him counseling. He just shut down. *This is not your fault.*"

"It's my fault that Frank Freeman was ever in our lives," she said bitterly.

"Without Frank there'd be no Aaron."

She shook her head. "It's my fault he showed up here and Aaron was forced to do what he did. I should've killed him when I had the chance the first time. You know why Aaron said he tried to... to kill himself? He said he's scared he's going to end up being like Frank. He said he'd rather be dead than end up like him."

I looked her in the eye. "We just have to convince him that that won't happen. We have to show him that his legacy is in being Scott Grant's son, *not* Frank's. We just have to convince him that he is good and that that man is not inside of him. I'll tell him. I'll tell him right now. Where is he?"

"He's locked up in a behavioral healthcare facility in Little Rock, on suicide watch," she said. Then she collapsed against me in tears. I held her to me tightly.

"Oh, Cleo. No wonder you're so worn out. You've been driving back and forth to see about him?"

She nodded.

"Why didn't you just tell me? Why would you keep this from me?"

"Because I was ashamed of myself," she said through her sobs. "I still am."

I pulled her face around to look at me. "You have no reason to be. You're an excellent mother. Shoot, all of your kids have always known who their fathers are. You got me beat by a mile."

She laughed lightly. "Don't make me laugh."

"Look, he's alive. That's a good thing. The Lord sent Shane to protect him. Things could be worse, Cleo. All we've got to do is pray like mad women and trust that God will bring him through this. When can I see him?"

"Tomorrow."

"Good thing I packed a bag for me and Corey and the kids. I think we'll stay a few days if that's okay with you and Scott."

She wiped her face. "You came prepared, huh? You just knew

we'd make up?"

"No, but I knew you needed me, so if we hadn't made up, I was gonna stay anyway."

She rested her head on my shoulder. "I'm glad you're here, Mo."

"I'm glad I'm here, too."

22

"Soul Inspiration"

We went to visit Aaron as a family the next day and the day after that. We hugged him and loved on him and prayed for him—all of us, or at least as many of us as they'd allow to visit him at one time. And even in that little time we were able to spend with him, I could see the light in his eyes begin to brighten. There is truly nothing better than the love of your family to help you through a dark time.

On the third day, we let Cleo and her family go alone to visit him while me, Corey, and our two kids stayed behind. After we ate lunch, Corey and I sat on the back porch and shared a quilt while Sahib and Nia napped. It was peaceful and the quilt plus our body heat provided just enough warmth for us to be able to enjoy the view.

Cleo's back yard was huge. There was a chicken coop—of all things—a small greenhouse, a tool shed, and a huge barn. The small portion of land where Scott usually planted a garden was bare. Beyond the yard was a thicket of trees—a forest, really. To the right of her home were several acres of land—farmland where Scott and his workers planted crops. My sister's home was country living at its finest.

"Scott says there's a pond full of fish back in those woods. Maybe I'll go out there with him before we leave. See what I can catch," Corey said.

I looked over at him. "You like to fish? You never told me that."

"I've never been interested in it up until now. Scott says it's really relaxing."

"Oh, well go for it."

He reached for my hand and gave it a little squeeze. "I like it here."

I smiled. "I do, too."

We silently watched a deer dart out of and back into the woods.

"Would you wanna move here? I mean would you consider living somewhere like this one day?" he asked.

I turned and stared at him for a moment. "Well, I'd love being close to my sister and her family. Sahib's small enough that the move shouldn't be bad on him. He can go to school at Cleo's church and we can just meet Wasif halfway to exchange him. Nia will be fine. Sure, I'd be thrilled, but are you serious? What about our business and our new house. What about our church and all of your friends?"

"The club can run itself as long as we keep a good staff. That's what it's been doing since I've been down anyway. Shoot, maybe we could even open another club here. Scott says there's definitely a market for it. And the house? We can sell it or rent it out. I really like Scott's church, and I can make new friends. Did you know that Scott and your sister own 500 acres of land? They own the forest back there, too. He owns the pond and basically his own hunting ground! He said he'd give us some land if we wanted. Or he'd help us find a place out here." Corey sounded so excited, more excited than he'd been in a long time.

"Sounds like you and Scott have things all worked out."

"I feel better here, baby. I feel stronger. I can breathe easier. I think being here would do us both some good."

I thought about what he said. Maybe we'd be far enough from Wasif that Corey wouldn't perceive him as a threat. And it would be better for Corey not to have to drive by the high school and relive the shooting nearly every day.

"When would you want to make the move?" I asked.

"I figure we should let Sahib finish out the school year. We can move some time in the summer. That should give us enough time to arrange everything and find somewhere here to live."

I nodded. "Okay."

"Really, baby?"

"Yeah, it'll be good to be close to family. I love the idea."

Corey pulled me close to him. I was excited about the idea. I would be so happy to live closer to my baby sister and her family. I stared out at the barn and thought about my ill-fated horse riding lesson and smiled. Then I remembered something else about the barn.

I kissed Corey on the cheek. "This trip was a great idea if I do say so myself."

"It was an excellent idea, baby."

***

Four boxes.

That was all that was left of our mother.

Four boxes.

As Cleo and I sat on her living room floor with the boxes in front of us, I wondered what we would find. Mama's friend, Dulcina, had packed up her things and driven them to Cleo's house. They'd been stashed in the barn for two years. They smelled like hay, and though this was my idea, I was almost afraid to open them.

"You really think this'll help?" Cleo asked.

"Help you find your father? Maybe. Help us learn more about Mama? I hope so."

She nodded.

We sat there together and stared at those boxes like they were a TV show or a movie. Finally, Cleo opened one of them and peered inside.

"Just books," she said.

She slid the box to the side and opened the other three boxes. She released a frustrated sigh. "All books!"

I frowned as I grabbed one of the boxes and pulled it to me. I began to empty its contents—*Treasure Island, Moby Dick, Little Women.* Our mother was nothing if not well read.

"I'm sorry, Cleo. I didn't mean to disappoint you. I just thought…"

Cleo shook her low-hung head. "It's okay. I knew better than to get my hopes up."

I knew how she felt. I absently opened my mother's copy of *Moby Dick* and as I thumbed through it, my eyes widened. "It's a journal," I whispered.

"You say something?" Cleo asked.

I dropped *Moby Dick* and picked up *Treasure Island*, then *Lord of the Flies*. I shoved *Little Women* into Cleo's face. "They're not books! They're her journals!! She glued these book covers onto them to disguise them! Look!"

Cleo flipped through the book, her eyes wide with wonder. Then we grabbed each other and hugged and giggled like we'd just discovered a buried treasure, like we'd uncovered some delightful secret.

We spent the next hour organizing the books by the dates written inside. Then, after eating lunch with our family, we begged them not to disturb us and we sat down and began to read our mother's words aloud to each other.

"I was born September 5, 1960 in England, Arkansas. My mother is white. My father is black, and me? I'm nothing."

That's how the very first entry in the first journal began. And the remainder of her words read similarly—like she was chronicling her life for someone. Was that what she'd done? Did she know that one day Cleo and I would be reading her words, her life's story?

We read and read until a small crowd of our husbands and children appeared in the living room, inquiring about dinner. And after we both gave them *the look*, they decided amongst themselves that pizza delivery would be just fine.

We read well into the night and learned about our mother's childhood. The stories of her life were horrible and heartbreaking. In reading this account of her life written in her own hand, I understood her anger, though it was very misdirected. I felt her pain. I wished I truly knew the woman who wrote these words. I wished she'd opened up to us.

We took breaks for dinner and after Corey appeared in the doorway with Nia in his arms and a worn look on his face, we halted our reading for the night. But we started back up right after breakfast the next morning.

Our mother had chronicled nearly every event of her life—some significant, others mundane. But it all gave us a better view of who Christina Dandridge was as a person. And I couldn't stop reading or listening to Cleo read. The more I read, the more I wanted to read, the more I wanted to know.

What was to be a quick trip to West Memphis and back to Conway stretched into a full week and a half of me and Cleo studying our mother's life and Scott and Corey bonding over fishing and illegal hunting. But Cleo and I were too enthralled by our mother's life story to worry about them being arrested for hunting out of season. I read with Nia on my hip or Sahib in my lap. Then I met Wasif in Little Rock on the way to visit Aaron one day so that he could keep Sahib and get him to and from school. And then I read some more.

By the middle of week two, Corey and I decided that as much as we loved being at my sister's place, it was time for us to go home. Cleo and I would divide the journals and keep each other posted on what new things we learned about our mother. We spent my last night there reading together, of course, and we found something absolutely incredible in one of the journals—Cleo's birth certificate. And along with it, a photo of a man cradling a baby. In the back were the words, *Donald and Cleopatra*.

Cleo stared at the picture with tears in her eyes. "This is my father."

From what I could see of her father's face, he looked very handsome. Cleo resembled him. "Hey, I think I remember him. He was nice. Really nice to me. I think I liked him," I said as I studied the photo.

Cleo nodded and then read the birth certificate. "His name was Donald Deroy Williams. He was 30. This will help. I just know it will!" She reached over and hugged me.

I was so happy for her. I was happy for both of us. Finding those journals was like stepping back in time. They made things so much easier to understand. They made our mother human in our eyes for the first time.

***

"Hey, it's Mo. Can I talk to you for a moment?" I said once Wasif answered the phone—a few days after we'd returned home.

"I don't know, can you?" he said sarcastically.

I sighed. "Yes, I can. Look, it's about Sahib."

"What about him? Did something happen? Is he okay?"

"He's fine, he's fine. I just wanted you to know that Corey and I are thinking about moving out of town next summer. It won't change the visitation schedule or anything. We're thinking of moving to be closer to my sister, but we can always meet halfway to trade off Sahib like we did the other day. I just wanted to give you a heads up."

"This is because of me, isn't it?"

"No, Wasif. Contrary to your belief, all of my decisions are not centered on my relationship with you."

"It feels like punishment."

"It's not. It's not about you *at all*. It's about what's best for my family. Look, I knew this would upset you. And please don't start that mess about custody because I will bury you before I let you take my baby boy from me."

Silence.

"Do you hear me?"

"I wish I understood you."

I closed my eyes and sucked in a breath as I tightened my grip on the phone. "Wasif..."

"No, listen. You just told me you're taking my boy away. The least you can do is *listen*."

"Fine."

"Don't do this. I accept that you love him more than you love me. I accept that you're not going to leave him for me. I accept that I can never have you all to myself again. I understand that I messed up. I get it; you've proven your point. But I need to be able to see you, Mo. I need at least that. *Don't do this*."

"Wasif, this is not about you. This is something Corey and I want and need. I'm sorry."

"Mo... Okay, fine. Whatever."

"Bye, Wasif."

"Bye."

23

"Moondance"

Corey and I, along all of our kids—including the twins—returned to my sister's house a week later to celebrate Christmas with them. Aaron was home and he looked and seemed better. He was continuing therapy on an outpatient basis.

When we made it to their house, he seemed genuinely happy to see his twin cousins. They were close in age and I hoped they would grow closer and be able to support one another as they grew further into adulthood. Cleo and I quickly settled into her living room and caught up on what we'd read in our mother's journals. She'd continued her search for her father but still had not been able to locate him. I had spoken to my father a couple of times on the phone but hadn't seen him in person since my last meltdown.

While we caught up and Serenity doted on Nia, the men, including Sahib, congregated in the backyard and watched a shooting competition between Scott and Aaron.

"Aaron can shoot the head off of an ant. Scott knows he's gonna lose," Cleo said.

I shrugged. "Maybe he's trying to help boost Aaron's confidence," I offered.

"Maybe so."

We took a break from our reading to have dinner and open presents with our families, and then we read all the way up until bedtime.

***

At first, I wasn't sure what woke me up. The guest bedroom where we slept was still and quiet so I just laid there and listened. Then I heard it. It was the faint cry of someone who sounded terrified. I looked over at Corey, who was fast asleep, then at Sahib and Nia who were asleep between us. I heard it again and decided to ease out of bed. It sounded like my sister's voice, and I needed to know what was going on.

I walked through the huge, old house in my gown and robe and made my way up the stairs. I was met in the upstairs hallway by Serenity.

"Mama's having another dream," she said, her eyes full of concern. "She hasn't had one in a while."

I wrapped my arm around her shoulder. "It'll be okay." But even as I said the words, I felt my own anxiety take hold of me. She was my sister. If she hurt, I hurt. "Go back to bed, sweetie," I said. "I'll check on her."

The beautiful thirteen-year-old, who already matched my height, nodded then turned and walked back into her room. Almost simultaneously, Aaron and Shane appeared in their doorways.

"Go back to bed guys. Everything's okay," I assured them, though I had no confidence in my own words.

Shane backed into his room almost as soon as the words left my mouth. Aaron hesitated and I saw something flash in his eyes.

"Aaron, I'll check on her. Don't worry."

He dropped his eyes. "I don't feel bad for killing him," he whispered. "Sometimes I think that makes me a bad person—like *him*. But when Mama gets like this, I think what I did was right."

I walked over to him and pulled him into a hug. I'd only known my nephew a little over five years and he'd never really opened up to me before. He'd never really opened up to anyone, at least not about this. I released him and reached up and cradled his handsome face in my hands—a face that was much like his father's, according to my sister.

"Aaron, listen. You did the only thing you could do in that situation. It's not like he was standing on some street corner minding his own business. He invaded your home. He had tried to kill your father, was about to kill your mother. He would've hurt your brother and sister. You did nothing more than protect your family. Anyone else would've done the same thing in a similar situation. You *shouldn't* feel bad about that."

He nodded. "Thanks. I just hope God can forgive me. I think about that a lot, you know, how God feels about what I did and how I don't feel bad about it."

"God was there, Aaron. He saw the whole thing. It was Him who led you back into the house to protect your family."

His eyes widened. "You think so?"

"I *know* so. Do you think it would've been His will for him to kill your parents or hurt your sister and brother?"

He shook his head slowly. "No."

"You are a prodigy with a gun, if there is such a thing. You think that's by accident?"

His eyes changed, as if I'd just given him a new revelation. "No, I guess not."

"See, what you did was the right thing in that situation. Don't forget that, Aaron. Don't *ever* forget that."

He nodded and backed into his room. "Thanks, Aunt Mo."

"You're welcome."

I continued down the hall to my sister's bedroom and knocked lightly on the door. Scott opened it and stepped out into the hall.

"Is everything okay?" I asked.

"Um, yeah, she's calmer, now."

"Can I come in?"

"No, it'd kill her for you to see her like this. I've got it handled. She'll be fine."

"Okay, let me know if you need me."

He nodded and then ducked back into the room.

As I headed back toward the stairs, Aaron's voice stopped me in my tracks.

"Aunt Mo?" he whispered almost conspiratorially. I turned around to find him standing in the middle of the hallway.

"Yes, Aaron?"

"I... I think I messed up."

I moved closer to him. "I told you, sweetheart, what you did was right."

He shook his head. "No, not that. It's Morgan."

My heart jumped in my chest. "What... what about Morgan?"

"Earlier, I gave him my gun and the keys to my truck. Blair is still in my room asleep. But Morgan, he's... he's gone."

24

"Rules"

I sat in the passenger's seat of my husband's SUV, wringing my hands and biting my bottom lip. We were more than halfway home with Blair and Aaron, who'd insisted on coming with us, in the backseat. I hated leaving Nia and Sahib behind, but I was afraid of what we'd see when we found Morgan, *if* we found him. Oh, how I hoped we'd find him before he did something horrible.

"He's still not answering," Blair, who'd been marathon calling Morgan's cell phone, said.

I looked over at Corey whose eyes were glued to the highway before us. He had a look of deep concentration on his face. He hadn't said a word since we left my sister's house.

"I'm sorry, Aunt Mo, Uncle Corey," Aaron said for the millionth time.

"It's... it's all right, Aaron," I said. But that was a lie if I'd ever told one. It *wasn't* okay. It was the worst thing he could've done giving Morgan a weapon *and* a vehicle. But I couldn't say that to someone fresh off of suicide watch. And honestly, I was too worried about Morgan to reprimand anyone, anyway.

"I need to call Wasif," I said as I eyed Corey. He nodded, his eyes still on the road.

Wasif sounded even more upset than I felt. He said he'd get out and drive around to see if he could find Morgan or Aaron's truck, which I'd described to him. But he had no clue where to look just like I didn't. But like me, he had to do *something* to try and find our son.

I hung up and clutched the phone tightly as I closed my eyes and prayed. Morgan was about to do something that would ruin his entire life. Unlike Aaron, what he was trying to do was unwarranted. He was seeking revenge—plain and simple.

A while later, we entered the Conway city limits and I watched as Corey turned onto a street and slowed down as if he knew exactly where he was going. I was curious but I kept my silence. He'd been calm so far—calmer than me, as a matter of fact. And to be honest, that scared me.

Corey slowed the car down to a snail's pace and I glanced into the back seat at the confused faces of my son and nephew. Then I looked back over at Corey who stopped the car in front of a house.

I couldn't hold my tongue any longer. "Baby, where are we?"

"Gary Webber's house."

I stared at him for a moment and wondered if I'd heard him right. Gary Webber was the name of the boy who'd shot him. "How do you know where he lives?" I asked.

He looked over at me. "His mother. She reached out to me a few weeks back. Called and left a message on my phone. She got my number from Frederick's wife. She... she said she wanted to apologize for what her son had done. I didn't tell you about it because I just didn't wanna think about it."

"She gave you her address on the message?"

"No. I called her when you were saying goodbye to your sister, right before we left. She wants to help."

I turned and looked at the house. Nothing felt right about this. "I don't know how I feel about this, Corey. Maybe we should just call the police."

Corey shook his head. "They'll arrest Morgan on the spot. Is that what you want?"

"You know it's not. But what if this is a trap or something?"

He looked over at me and shook his head. "I don't think it is, baby. I think she's sincerely sorry for what her son did. I think she'll help us find him and, hopefully, Morgan."

I shook my head. "Don't do this."

Corey sighed. "You got a better idea, Mona? I mean, what are we gonna do? Drive around town and hope that Morgan parked Aaron's truck somewhere in plain sight. He might be doing something stupid right now, but he's not *dumb*. He's probably hidden that truck." He reached over and placed his hand over mine. "This is the best chance we've got."

I sighed as I opened the truck door. "Okay, let's go."

"No. You stay here." He glanced at the boys. "*All of you* stay here. I'll be right back."

Before either of us could protest, Corey opened his door and climbed out of the car. As I watched him walk toward the house, I closed my eyes and began to pray.

***

Twenty minutes later, I was still sitting in the car, teetering on insanity. My eyes were glued to the house. My ears were standing at attention—listening. Listening for what? A scream, a gunshot? I rocked back and forth in my seat as I clutched my cell phone. A silent prayer constantly played in my head. *Please keep Corey safe. Please let Morgan be okay. Please help me, God.* I glanced back at Blair and Aaron who wore nearly identical worried faces.

"I'm sorry, Aunt Mo," Aaron whispered.

I didn't reply, couldn't offer him any more false reassurance—not at that moment. I just couldn't.

"It's okay, Aaron," Blair said.

Blair, the level-headed one. The one who never raised his voice or gave me a second's trouble. Why did my one and only son by Corey have to be so bullheaded? Why, why, why?

My phone rang, interrupting my pointless thoughts. It was Wasif.

"Hello?" I answered.

"What kind of truck did you say he was in? I think I might've found it," said Wasif.

"What?! Um, uh, it's a red Toyota Tacoma with mud flaps and a vanity plate on the back." My heart was about to explode in my chest. Could he really have found him?

"Does the vanity plate say Aaron?"

I nodded vigorously. "Yes! Yes, that's it! Where is it? Where is he?" I glanced into the back seat to see Blair opening his door.

"I'll get Coach," he said. A relieved look spread across Aaron's face.

"Behind the high school. He hid it pretty well, almost didn't see it. I'm gonna see if I can find him on the campus," Wasif said.

"Oh, thank you! Thank God! We'll be right there."

"All right. See you in a bit."

I hung up and closed my eyes and thanked God over and over again. When I opened them, I could see Blair and Corey approaching the car. Moments later, we were all headed to Conway High School.

***

My feet were numb as I stepped out of the truck onto the parking lot outside Conway High School and waited for Corey. He sat in the car for a few moments, doing something with his phone, before climbing out of the truck and walking around to join me. My hand shook as he took it and squeezed it in his.

"Should we split up?" Blair asked.

"No," said Corey.

We were silent as he led us around the campus—behind buildings and across parking lots. He tried several doors, all locked. And though we'd seen both Wasif's car on the lot and Aaron's truck behind one of the buildings, there was no sign of either Wasif or Morgan anywhere on that campus. It was eerily quiet except for the sound of our footsteps as we embarked on a seemingly pointless search. Then Corey stopped in his tracks and looked at us. His eyes widened.

"The gym," he said. "They're in the gym."

I shook my head. "We tried that door. It was locked, remember? All of the doors are locked. And even if they did manage to get inside one of the buildings, wouldn't the alarm have gone off? Wouldn't the police be here by now?"

"No," he said as he turned and began walking toward the gym. "Frederick once told me that only certain buildings have alarm systems—the ones with a lot of computers and stuff. I remember him saying how crazy that was. The gym has no alarm. Neither does the field house. And no, we didn't try *all* of the gym doors."

"That was then, baby. How do you know they don't have alarms now?" I asked as I tried to match his determined stride.

"We'll see. They gotta be somewhere on this campus and they aren't out here."

I sighed and continued to follow him to the gym doors—a set on the side of the building that we hadn't tried. And then Corey just stopped. He just stopped and stood there as if all of the determination he'd just displayed had disappeared into thin air. He just stood there and stared at the door.

"Coach? Is it locked?" Blair asked after he and Aaron caught up with us.

Corey didn't answer.

I softly rested my hand on his arm. He jerked away from me and slowly turned to look at me. "I just realized that this is where it happened. I haven't been back. I take these crazy routes through town to avoid this whole campus. *This is where it happened.*"

"Why don't we just call the police, baby? No one expects you to go back in there."

"No. I can do it. For Morgan." He paused, turned around, and looked at Blair. "For our children." He looked at me. "And for you. I can do this."

My tears came then. I nodded and watched as he slowly opened the gym door. No alarm sounded; only the loud groan of the rusty door hinges could be heard. As Corey slowly pulled the door open, I held my breath and watched his face. And when I saw his eyes widen, I followed his gaze into the gym. The only light in the huge space was the red glow of the exit signs that hung throughout the room and the scoreboard which proudly boasted the electric blue Wampus Cat mascot. My eyes had to adjust in the poorly lit room. But it didn't take long to see what Corey was staring at. There, on the other end of the gym, was my husband's assailant—on his knees, his head down. And our son, my oldest child, was standing there holding a gun to the young man's head.

25

"Sometimes"

Wasif stood to the side, not far from Morgan. His eyes were glued to me as I stepped into the gym behind Corey. He looked as afraid as I felt. And though the door groaned loudly as it slammed shut, Morgan never took his eyes off of Gary. And Gary never raised his head. Was he already dead? Had Morgan killed him?

Then I noticed that there was no blood. And I could see Gary's body shift a little.

"Morgan," Corey said, his eyes fixed on the young man who'd tried to end his life.

Morgan looked up with a startled expression. I think that maybe he actually hadn't heard us come in. But as quickly as he looked up at us, he looked back at Gary. Gary raised his head to reveal his swollen features, his bloodied face. It seemed that Morgan had already worked him over.

I gasped. "Morgan, what'd you do?"

"What I had to do," he said without taking his eyes off of Gary.

"Put the gun down, son. Come on. Put the gun down," Wasif said. His voice was hoarse. I had a feeling he'd been pleading with Morgan for quite a while.

"I know you're upset. But now that you've found him, let me call the police, baby. Don't do this," I said.

"Give me the gun, Morg," Blair said.

I looked over at Corey and at Aaron who stood right behind him. They wore almost duplicate expressions of terrified familiarity on their faces but neither of them said a word.

"Morgan," I said, "Morgan, don't do this."

"Everybody just be quiet! I can't think!" he shouted.

The hand that held the gun trembled. He wiped his brow. As cold as it was in that gym, he was sweating. He was nervous, maybe even a little afraid. That gave me a glimmer of hope. Maybe he was too nervous or afraid to actually pull the trigger.

I opened my mouth to speak again and then noticed Wasif shaking his head. His eyes shifted to Corey and back to me. I knew what he was thinking. Morgan would probably listen to Corey. I'd been thinking the same thing. But Corey was frozen and I was afraid to push him. I shut my mouth and gently placed my hand on Corey's arm. He jumped a little and looked at me. I nodded toward the scene in front of us and mouthed "say something." I could see the recognition in his eyes. He remembered why we were there.

"Morgan. Don't do this. It won't fix anything. It'll only make things worse," Corey said softly.

Morgan looked up at his father and shook his head. I could see tears shimmering in his eyes. "He tried to kill you."

"But, by the grace of God, *he didn't*. I'm here, Morgan. *I'm right here*. I know we haven't had a lot of time together as father and son, but we do have the rest of our lives. If you do this, you'll cut that time. I'll have to visit you in prison."

"At least he'll be gone. He don't deserve to live. You know why he did it? You wanna know what he told me after I beat it out of him?"

Corey hesitated. "It... it doesn't matter, Morgan."

"Yeah, it does. Tell him," he said as he lightly kicked the young man in the knee. The boy jerked but didn't speak. "Tell him!" Morgan shouted as he hit the boy in the head with the butt of the gun.

I covered my mouth with my hand. "Morgan, *please...*"

The boy looked up at us with exhaustion in his eyes. "Because Dominic Carter was messing with me."

I recognized Dominic as the name of one of the kids who was killed.

Morgan looked up at us. "This dude tried to kill *you* because some kid was messing with him. You ain't have nothing to do with that! He shoulda handled that mess one on one instead of shooting up the whole gym! That's just crazy!"

"Were you being bullied, Gary?" Corey asked. I suppose he was trying to make some sense of what happened.

"That don't matter!" Morgan shouted. "*You* didn't bully him! Neither did Coach Frederick or those other kids he shot!"

Corey nodded. "You're right, Morgan. He had no right to shoot up this gym. But you have no right to kill him, either. You're better than this, son. You're not this person. You're not the person who kills people. This is something you can't come back from. You'll never get over this. Give me the gun."

"No, I *gotta* do this. The police been looking for him for weeks but *I* found him and *I'm* gon' finish this right here and right now."

As he pressed the gun against the boy's temple, my knees began to shake and the sound of my own heartbeat was deafening in my ears. "Morgan, please, please, *please*, don't do this. *Please.* Please, don't!" I pleaded.

"It's gonna mess you up, man, like it did me. You ain't gonna be able to sleep or eat. You're gonna see his body every time you shut your eyes. You ain't gonna ever forget how it felt to pull that trigger. How it felt to watch that bullet hit him. How the blood smelled. You'll see him hit the floor over and over again. You won't ever forget what you did. And you'll never be the same," Aaron said. He moved close to Morgan. "I need my gun back, cuz."

Morgan shook his head and as he looked up at Aaron, a single tear rolled down his cheek. He adjusted his finger on the trigger. "No, I need to do this."

Aaron moved a little closer. "No, you don't, man. Believe me, this ain't what you want. I'm messed up. I did what I did to save my family and it *still* messed me up. But what you're doing? It ain't right. You need to let the law handle this dude. You're letting him off too easy by killing him. Let them lock his little tail up. Let the dudes in prison take care of him."

Gary moved his head slightly. Morgan pressed the gun deeper into his temple. We all stood there and waited. No more words were spoken, because there was nothing left to say. It was up to Morgan now, up to him to make the right choice.

I watched as more tears raced down his cheeks. And then he held the gun out toward Aaron. Aaron grabbed the gun and Wasif grabbed Morgan as he broke down in nearly inconsolable tears. As Blair walked over to Morgan and wrapped his arms around his father and brother, Corey followed him but stopped in front of Gary. Then he just stared down at him. Gary still hadn't lifted his head. I held my breath. What was Corey doing?

"Look at me," Corey said—no—*commanded.*

Gary didn't move.

"*Look at me,*" Corey repeated.

Gary slowly raised his head and looked up at Corey.

"You remember me?"

Gary nodded.

"Good. Now, I don't ever want you to forget what happened here tonight. How we spared your life. How we did better by you than you did by my friend and those children you murdered... and *me.*"

A sneer spread across Gary's face. "You shoulda let him kill me. Cause I ain't messed up 'bout none of them dead people or *you.*"

"I hope you realize what you've done and repent before it's too late. In the meantime, I'll be praying for you," Corey said.

Gary looked up at Corey and laughed. He doubled over and clutched his stomach and laughed like he was at a Kevin Hart show sitting front row center.

Corey shook his head as he backed away from him.

Morgan glared at Gary. "Y'all shoulda let me kill him."

"They-sho'-shoulda!" Gary snorted as he continued to laugh.

Morgan lunged for the young man but was held back by Blair and Aaron.

Then the gym doors flew open.

And Officer Mark walked in.

26

"No One To Blame"

I stood in the parking lot hiccupping and sniffling and trying not to grab ahold of my boy's ankles and drag him out of the police car. Officer Mark had arrested Gary then called for backup. The backup officer arrested Morgan. I knew he'd broken the law by assaulting Gary and threatening him with a gun, but the mother I was just couldn't accept that my boy, the boy I'd fed and diapered, was being arrested.

I walked over to the police car and pressed my face against the window. I wailed and screamed my boy's name and begged the officer not to take him away. As I clawed at the cold window, I felt sets of hands grab me and pull me away—the hands of Blair and Aaron and Corey. Through my tears, I could see Wasif. I could see that he wanted to help me, that his heart ached for Morgan as well. I could see the tears and pain in his eyes. I could also see the love.

I tightly shut my eyes and sobbed loudly as the pain in my heart intensified. "No, please. Somebody do something. Somebody help him! *Please!*"

I could hear Corey saying something but I couldn't make out his words. Then, with blurred vision, I watched as Blair and Aaron left us and climbed inside Aaron's truck. Then Corey steered me to our vehicle.

"Come on, baby. We gotta go. Come on," he said softly.

I looked him in the eye as I tightly clutched his arms. "You gotta help him. He did this for you. You gotta help him."

Corey nodded. "I know, baby. I'm gonna help him, but we need to leave right now. Dr. Masood's getting him a lawyer. There's nothing else to do right now. We need to go get Sahib and Nia and get back here, okay? They say we might have to answer some more questions in the morning."

I slid into the car and watched as Wasif pulled off of the parking lot. Once Corey climbed in beside me, I said, "How can you be so calm?"

Corey started the car but didn't answer me.

"Corey, did you hear me?"

Still no answer.

"Corey—"

He jerked the car to a stop at the edge of the parking lot and turned to face me. It was then that I saw the tears streaming down his face. "What, Mona?! What? What do you want? I'm worried. I'm upset. I feel guilty. *This is all my fault.* I wish it was me in that police car! I'd give anything to take my son's place! Is this what you wanted?" He slammed his fist on the steering wheel. "You want me to break down?! I'm trying to hold it together so that I can drive back to your sister's house and get our other kids! You're not the only one hurting here! He's my son and I love him. Hell, Dr. Masood loves him! This is not just about *you*!"

I dropped my eyes. "I... I know that. I... I'm sorry."

He reached over and caressed my cheek. "Look, I'm sorry for yelling, Mona. Just... let's just not talk right now, okay?"

I nodded. "Okay."

I turned and fixed my eyes on the darkness outside my window. And I kept my mouth shut, crying silent tears all the way to my sister's house.

***

I couldn't visit Morgan in jail. I just couldn't. I could not bear to see him in there. He didn't deserve this. He had done what the police couldn't. He'd followed the clues, kept his ear to the street, and found a fugitive murderer. No, he didn't deserve to be in jail.

I spent nearly every waking moment of my life thinking about him and praying for mercy on his behalf and my own, because I honestly would not be able to take it they threw the book at him. But they did just that. My baby was charged with aggravated assault.

The lawyer Wasif hired was working on getting him bail. Corey spent nearly all of his time on the phone or at the police station trying to help Morgan. As for me, it was all I could do to hold on to my sanity and take care of Sahib and Nia. And when I wasn't taking care of them, I stayed in bed and tried to sleep the stress and anxiety away. It didn't work, of course. You can't sleep reality away. You can't make horrible things disappear by closing your eyes. But I tried.

My church prayed. Blair went back to school. The two men in my life worked hard. My youngest children were unaware. Life went on. But with every beat of my heart, I could feel myself falling apart more and more. Concerned phone calls from Cleo and my father helped. But nothing could really dull the ache of knowing that my oldest child, my precious boy, was in jail and alone.

Nothing.

27

"It's Been You"

Morgan pled guilty and was sentenced to probation because of the special circumstances surrounding the case. The judge said that in a lot of ways, Morgan was a hero. That he was not a bad person, but that he should remember in the future to let the police do their jobs and not take the law into his own hands. He would have to regularly report to his probation officer and perform community service. But he was nineteen, an adult. He now had a criminal record that would follow him for the rest of his life. And despite the fact that my father was his coach, he lost his scholarship and was expelled from the Christian college he and his brother attended. For the first time in their lives, he and Blair would be separated. Nevertheless, things could've been much worse. He could've received a prison sentence.

My entire body relaxed when I heard the sentence. I couldn't wait to hug my baby and take him home and cook him whatever he wanted. I never wanted him out of my sight again. I felt like I owed Wasif's lawyer my life. I felt like hugging and kissing every stranger on the street *and* his mama. My boy was coming home!

We were all happy and relieved. I could see it on Corey's and Wasif's faces. This tragedy was over. Morgan was about to be free. We could all breathe again.

***

A few days later, I was sitting in the kitchen talking to Morgan and watching him eat breakfast while he waited for Wasif to pick him up to enroll him in classes at a local college.

When the doorbell rang, I heard Corey yell, "I'll get it!" A few minutes later, both he and Wasif walked into the kitchen. Wasif held Sahib's hand and wore an awkward look on his face.

"Um, Morgan, can you excuse us for a moment?" Corey asked softly. "And take Sahib with you?"

Morgan sat there for a moment, confusion on his face. He looked over at me and I could see uncertainty in his eyes. We were both unsure about this situation. Corey and Wasif being in the same room together had never been a good situation. But I gave him a little nod and hoped I was doing the right thing. Morgan and Sahib left. Corey offered Wasif a seat and Wasif hesitantly sat down across from me. The only thought in my head was, *Did he tell Corey about that night in the hotel room?* My stomach churned. My heart raced.

Corey pulled a chair next to mine, sat down, and gripped my hand. Wasif shifted his eyes away from us. Corey cleared his voice. "I owe you an apology, Dr. Masood."

Wasif looked at Corey, then me. He frowned. "What?"

"For the way I acted after you did my surgery. I apologize and I want to thank you for saving my life. I know you only did it for Mona, but you still saved my life. So thank you."

Dang, those counseling sessions are the bomb, I thought.

Wasif shifted in his seat. "Um... well, I was just doing my job."

"Well, you did it well. Thanks to you, I get to raise my little girl and be here for the boys."

Wasif nodded. "Yeah, well, like you said, I did it for Mo."

Corey squeezed my hand. "You'd do anything for her, wouldn't you?"

My heart was beating with such force, I was afraid I was having a heart attack. "Corey—"

"Wouldn't you?" Corey repeated. "You still love her?"

Wasif dropped his eyes. "Very much so."

"And you want to be with her?" Corey asked.

Wasif nodded slightly. "More than anything."

"I can't give her up," Corey whispered.

Wasif stared at Corey. "I wouldn't expect you to. If I was in your shoes, I wouldn't either."

"Um, I'm sitting right here," I interjected.

"Will you let her go? Will you give me your word that you'll move on?" Corey asked, ignoring my statement.

Wasif was quiet.

"Corey," I began. "Where is this coming from? There's nothing between us."

"He ended his engagement, right? I know that was because of you. I need for him to move on because I know that he's a weakness for you. I've always known it. I just can't accept it anymore. If I'm gonna get past this anger, I need his word, as a man, that he'll move on."

I looked Corey in the eye. "A *weakness*? Corey—"

"Don't bother denying it. I see it in your eyes when he walks into the room. I see it *right now*. And I know it's only a matter of time before something happens and the problem is, you are *my* weakness, Mona. I love you despite myself. I love you despite the things you do. But if it happens again, I can't be with you. I don't want to lose you. Not after all I've been through, all *we've* been through."

"You won't lose me, Corey. I promise you that. I love you, too. I'll never hurt you again."

"I know you love me and you wouldn't purposely hurt me. But I also know that there's this… *thing* between you and him. I need for it to end and I need for it to end *today*."

Wasif cleared his voice. "Can I speak to her alone?"

After a few moments of uncomfortable silence, Corey stood from the table and left the kitchen without a word.

I waited a few minutes and then whispered, "Did you tell him about what happened in the hotel room?"

"So he can kill me? No!" Wasif whispered back.

I raised my voice to a reasonable volume. "What do you need to talk to me about?"

"Um, I've met someone else. Her name is Stacy. She's an author. She's a lot like you but she's also different from any woman I've ever known, if that makes sense, and I really like her. She's smart and funny. I think I'm ready to move on and start a relationship with her."

I felt a little twinge of jealousy but ignored it. "Well, good for you, Wasif."

"Look, I need you to tell me right now if there's any chance of us being together. If not, I think I can have a future with her."

I smiled. "The way you talk about her, sounds like you've already moved on."

"You didn't answer my question."

"No, Wasif. No chance," I said softly.

He gave me a slight smile and his eyes told me what I'm sure he was afraid to say while sitting in Corey's house. My eyes reciprocated. We loved each other, always would. But my place was with my husband. Our eyes told each other that we understood that.

Wasif shifted his gaze to the table. "Uh, me and Morgan should head out now."

I nodded. "Sure, let me get him for you."

After Morgan and Wasif left, Corey joined me in the kitchen.

"Is it over now?" he asked.

"It's *been* over, Corey."

Corey looked me in the eye. *"Is it over now?"*

I stared at him. *He knew.* I could feel that somehow he knew what had happened, that I'd been holding on to feelings for Wasif.

"Yes, it's over now," I said softly.

"Good."

28

"Love You To The Letter"

I repositioned myself in the bed and adjusted the phone on my ear. "So how's everything going? How are Scott and the kids?"

"They're great. Everyone's keeping busy. Aaron's so much better; he's even decided to start taking some classes at the local college. Shane's got a girlfriend and Serenity is giving him hell about it."

I laughed. "Sounds about normal."

"How about you? Are you sure you're gonna do this? You've made up your mind?"

"Yeah. It's the right thing to do. Just found out I'm a match."

"I think it's a wonderful thing to do. What made you change your mind?"

"Reading Mama's journals and getting to know her and understand her through her own words. I wish she'd reached out to us, tried to bond with us. My father—at least he's trying. If I give him one of my kidneys, we'll have more time to get to know each other. Or at least I hope we will. I pray he doesn't just disappear after the surgery. I guess that's just a chance I'll have to take."

"And you're a match? I'd say that God is definitely in this plan."

"Well, I'm his only child, as far as he knows. I'm his only chance and, as hard as I can be, I'd feel bad if he died and I could've helped him."

"I'm proud of you, Mo. How are Corey and the kids?"

"They're good. Nia just turned seven months old and she's crawling up a storm, follows Sahib around the house like he's her idol. He loves it, though. Blair's good, got a new girlfriend. I can tell Morgan misses being in Mississippi, but he's making the most of things here. Corey's watching him like a hawk. We still plan on moving, eventually, but Corey doesn't want to leave Morgan right now."

"I can understand that. How's Corey's health?"

"He's good. Totally off of oxygen now. He's even started working out a little bit and working at the gym a couple of days a week."

"Good. I'm glad. Look, I'm sorry about all that stuff I said about him."

"Don't be. You were just concerned and you don't know him like I do. I understood where you were coming from but I just couldn't give up on him."

"I'm glad you didn't."

"Me, too. Hey, any progress with the search for your father?"

She sighed. "Nope, none."

"I'm sorry, Cleo. Don't give up. I know you'll find him."

"Yeah, well, it'd be nice if he just fell into my lap like your father did."

"You never know. Maybe he'll need a vital organ one day soon, too."

"That was mean."

"But it was true."

"I guess so. Did you ever find anything about our uncle in your set of Mama's journals?"

"Nothing. You?"

"No, I didn't. It's like she erased him or something."

"Yeah, it is. It's a mystery for sure."

"Well, I'm gonna get off now. Scott just walked in with a cooler full of something for me to cook. Love you, Mo."

"Love you, too."

I hung up and climbed out of bed. I made my way to the living room where Nia and Sahib were flanking Corey on the sofa, all three of them engrossed in an episode of *Spongebob*. Faithful Lizzie was sitting at his feet. I walked over to Corey and sat in his lap.

He smiled up at me as he wrapped his arms around me. I returned his smile and kissed him softly on the lips.

"What was that for?" he asked.

"No reason other than I love you."

Corey pushed my hair behind my ear and looked into my eyes. "I love you, too, baby."

Are you a victim of a violent crime needing counseling or other assistance? If so, visit:

http://www.victimsofcrime.org/help-for-crime-victims/find-local-assistance---connect-directory

To learn more about PTSD (Post-Traumatic Stress Disorder), visit:

http://www.helpguide.org/mental/post_traumatic_stress_disorder_symptoms_treatment.htm

To learn more about the author, visit:

http://adriennethompsonwrites.webs.com

To join Adrienne's mailing list, sign up here:

http://eepurl.com/jnDmH

Follow Adrienne on Twitter!

https://twitter.com/A_H_Thompson

Like Adrienne on Facebook!

https://www.facebook.com/AdrienneThompsonWrites

Follow Adrienne on Pinterest!

http://www.pinterest.com/ahthompsn/

Want to learn more about Mona's mother? Check out this excerpt from

September (The Christina Dandridge Story)

Coming in 2015

Hands, knees, and eyes on the floor. Hands, knees, and eyes on the floor.

Those words, words I'd heard over and over again, screamed in my head.

Hands, knees, and eyes on the floor.

Whack!

I knew the sound of Uncle Teddy's belt hitting flesh as well as I knew the sound of water running in the tub or pee streaming into a toilet. I knew it too well. And I knew that either one of my cousins or my brother, Kenny, had eyeballed him. We'd been on our knees for hours now, practicing the cardinal rules of my uncle's house.

1. Bow when he enters the room.

2. Stay in that position until he leaves the room.

3. Never, ever look him in the eye.

I was smart, so I hardly ever broke the rules. And anyway, if I didn't look at him, maybe he wouldn't see the hatred in my eyes. I hated him. I hated his home. I hated his weak wife and his evil children. I hated my mother for leaving me there. I hated my father for not caring enough to rescue me. I hated everything.

"Kenny Ray! Your little half-black behind is gonna learn to follow my rules! Or else I'm gonna beat the rebellious nigger out of you!"

Whack!

I could hear Kenny whimpering. He knew not to cry out. He knew that would only make things worse. I squeezed my eyes tightly shut and willed myself not to look at my baby brother. Because if I looked at him, I knew I would have to do something to help him.

Whack!

"You hear me, Kenny Ray?! I told your damn mama to stop sneaking around with the hired help. But did she listen? No! Just kept right on sneaking 'round my mama and daddy's farm with him. Hiding out in barns and letting him have his way with her and what did it get her? He's gone and she's stuck with you two mud puppies. Now she done left you two on me because her new husband don't want you. I let you into my house and how do you repay my kindness? By breaking my rules!"

Whack!

I gritted my teeth.

"I'm… I'm sorry, Uncle Teddy," Kenny Ray said softly.

"Did I say you could speak, nigger?!"

Whack!

I covered my ears with my hands, felt Uncle Teddy's feet shift on the weak floor.

"Hands, knees, and eyes, Chrissy!" he shouted, his attention on me now.

I quickly slapped my hands back onto the floor.

Whack!

The belt hit the small of my back and my knees buckled. I could hear soft snickering beside me. No doubt it was my cousin, Carrie.

Whack!

Now Carrie began to whimper. At least he was an equal opportunity abuser. His kids got as bad as me and Kenny Ray did.

Excerpt from

Locked Out Of Heaven—A Bluesday Continuation (Tomeka's Story)

Coming Summer 2014

Prologue

Rio Grande River—Texas/Mexico Border

I sat there and tried to catch my breath but I was too scared to breathe. Too scared to think. I was trembling but was it from the cold, night air that seemed to instantly freeze my wet clothes and skin, or was it from the fear, the terror?

"We gotta keep moving," he said. "Come on, we gotta keep moving. I promise we'll take a break as soon as it's safe."

He reached for my hand and helped me up from the ground. We ran and ran and ran. The sound of the barking dogs made my heart race faster than it should have. And then there was another sound—gun shots. One after the other. I screamed as I covered my ears and continued to run. Tears wet my face, almost burning my skin in the freezing cold. I ran until I ran out of both breath and strength. Then I dove into some bushes.

"I'm sorry," I whispered. "I can't go any further."

No answer. It was then that I realized I was alone. Where was he?

Seconds later, I heard a scream. A horrible scream. It was him. They'd caught him.

www.ingramcontent.com/pod-product-compliance
Lightning Source LLC
Chambersburg PA
CBHW060921250626
47159CB00008B/3102